"I want to learn from the best," Tacy said.

Brent waited for her to say more.

"I could leave here today, head down to any number of ranches I know of where I could learn to break horses. There are a lot of talented cowboys."

Everything she said was the truth, Brent knew. She could go learn to break horses anywhere. She was good enough, that was certain—he admitted it. Still, if he put Tacy on that horse and something happened it would be his responsibility.

"But," Tacy continued, studying him hard, "I believe we've met for a reason. I can feel it. I think maybe God has brought us together for a reason—*other* than for you to aggravate me."

Books by Debra Clopton

Love Inspired

*The Trouble with
  Lacy Brown
*And Baby Makes Five
*No Place Like Home
*Dream a Little Dream
*Meeting Her Match
*Operation: Married
  by Christmas

*Next Door Daddy
*Her Baby Dreams
*The Cowboy Takes a Bride
*Texas Ranger Dad
Small-Town Brides
"A Mule Hollow Match"
*His Cowgirl Bride

*Mule Hollow

DEBRA CLOPTON

was a 2004 Golden Heart finalist in the inspirational category, a 2006 Inspirational Readers' Choice Award winner, a 2007 Golden Quill award winner and a finalist for the 2007 American Christian Fiction Writers Book of the Year Award. She praises the Lord each time someone votes for one of her books, and takes it as an affirmation that she is exactly where God wants her to be.

Debra is a hopeless romantic and loves to create stories with lively heroines and the strong heroes who fall in love with them. But most importantly she loves showing her characters living their faith, seeking God's will in their lives one day at a time. Her goal is to give her readers an entertaining story that will make them smile, hopefully laugh and always feel God's goodness as they read her books. She has found the perfect home for her stories writing for the Love Inspired line and still has to pinch herself just to see if she really is awake and living her dream.

When she isn't writing, she enjoys taking road trips, reading and spending time with her two sons, Chase and Kris. She loves hearing from readers and can be reached through her Web site, www.debraclopton.com, or by mail at P.O. Box 1125, Madisonville, Texas 77864.

His Cowgirl Bride
Debra Clopton

Steeple
Hill®

Published by Steeple Hill Books™

STEEPLE HILL BOOKS

Steeple
Hill®

Recycling programs
for this product may
not exist in your area.

ISBN-13: 978-0-373-81441-1

HIS COWGIRL BRIDE

www.SteepleHill.com

Printed in U.S.A.

And the God of all grace, who called you to His eternal glory in Christ, after you have suffered a little while, will Himself restore you and make you strong, firm and steadfast.

—1 *Peter* 5:10

This book is dedicated to Tacy W. Thank you so much for lending me your first name and also your sunny smile as the inspiration for Tacy Jones, the heroine of this book! And also, to all my nieces: Alisha, Becky, Rikki Lyn, Dani Kay and Mariah. Y'all's Texas spunk and beauty always inspire me to write strong young women as my heroines. Last but not least, this book is dedicated to Bryleigh Belle M., whose sassy smile and darling name inspired Haley Bell Thornton's name in my book *Operation: Married by Christmas*. You are all beautiful young women inside and out... may God bless you all.

I'd also like to thank my editor, Krista Stroever, for her continued dedication and much valued input into all of my books. To editorial assistant Shana Smith, for all the things you do in the publishing process— thank you so much! And to the great team at Steeple Hill and Harlequin Books—I'm blessed to be a part of this group.

Chapter One

"Stay, Birdy," Tacy Jones told her blue-heeler as the truck carrying six colts in need of saddle breaking pulled up the drive. The driver gave her a thumbs-up when she waved and pointed toward the corral next to the barn. He swung the long trailer around in the dusty yard, then backed up to the gates. Dry dirt rose around the wheels as the heavy trailer came to a halt. Tacy jumped from the porch and jogged toward the corral as Birdy tore across the yard.

At the edge of the trailer, Birdy dropped to the ground and waited. Working cattle or horses was in the dog's blood, but she wouldn't act unless given the go-ahead. Like Tacy, she watched the horses stirring inside the trailer.

"Not today, girl," Tacy said, standing at the back of the trailer. "Looks like a good group," she called as the stout driver rolled out of the cab and headed past her to open the doors.

"Yeah, that's what I thought when I picked them up in Amarillo. They're not real fond of people, though. Even halter-broke like they are, they're trouble."

"They look a little jumpy. You want me to help lead them out?" Tacy asked.

The driver held up a hand for her to halt. "No can do, little lady. They're my responsibility 'til I get 'em outta my trailer. After that they're all yours. Not a minute sooner." He added the last sentence with the finality of a slammed door.

"Not exactly mine," Tacy mumbled, frustrated that all she was supposed to do was feed and water the beautiful animals until Pace and Sheri returned from Australia. A glorified babysitter—well, horse sitter—was all Tacy was supposed to be at her friends' ranch for the next several weeks. No way would she be able to stand this! She watched the driver struggle to lead the skittish animals forward. Like old yard dogs fighting against wearing a leash, the colts locked their knees one moment and backed away from him the next. Birdy kept looking up at Tacy with questioning eyes, and Tacy could only shake her head. By the time the man *finally* led the last colt off the trailer, he was clearly embarrassed. *As he should be!* She tried not to feel vindicated—but she was and there was no getting around it. Tacy wouldn't have had such a struggle and she knew it. She might not know how to fully break horses yet, but she had trained some. *Men*—they thought they knew everything. She could have told him that all he had to do was remove the halters in the trailer and the colts would make a mad dash for freedom. Which they did, heading straight toward the far end of the corral once the man let them loose.

Sweating and as pink as rose petals, the truck driver slammed the trailer door shut. "Now you can have them," he grunted and, without so much as a "Have a nice day," hoisted himself back into the driver's seat and hauled out of the yard like he was being chased by wolves.

Tacy shook her head and climbed up to perch on the top rung of the corral, then returned her attention to the horses. They stood at the far end, huddled together in a tight group. Though Pace had already told her they were from good stock, it was easy to tell just by looking at them. Their proportions were perfect, their muscles well-defined. They really were beauties. Two roans, a feisty chestnut, a midnight black and a paint. She loved the look of the paint—she was partial to chocolate-swirl ice cream, too.

Quietly, she studied them, holding a hand out, wanting to touch them even though they weren't coming near her. "By the time Pace and Sheri get back, we'll be friends," she said soothingly. Horses were some of the most beautiful and interesting animals God had created, as far as Tacy was concerned. She'd been infatuated with them since she was a toddler and hadn't ever wanted to be anything except a trainer—if she'd been a son instead of a daughter, that dream wouldn't have required a move here for Pace to help her bring it to fruition. Nope, she could have learned the business right alongside her four brothers. However, being the only girl in the family…well, it was complicated, so here she was at her friends' ranch, determined to make her future what *she* wanted it to be. Not what others dictated. She had come here three weeks ago, champing at the bit herself—eager for Pace to teach her how to break horses. But he and Sheri had gotten called away to the ranch in Australia, and here Tacy sat, her dream on hold until they returned.

Soon, she thought with a sigh. Food and a gentle word to get them used to her would be a start.

"Nothing like the present to start a good thing." She climbed down from the fence, slow and easy so as not to startle them, and went and filled a bucket with feed.

She'd just entered the pen when a blue Silverado with a matching horse trailer pulled into the drive. Giving the wary horses a wistful glance, Tacy opened the gate and went to see who had arrived.

Almost before the truck came to a halt, a cowboy with a Stetson pulled low over his brow leaped from the cab. Tall, broad-shouldered, he had her attention immediately—even before he plucked the hat from his head and she realized exactly who it was. By the time Brent Stockwell came to a halt, Tacy's heart had skipped a few beats and tumbled to her toes.

"What do you think you're doing?" he demanded, his expression tight as he glared from her to the horses.

"Excuse me?" The fact that Mr. Famous Bronc-buster-extraordinaire was standing smack in front of her, asking rude questions, had her reeling. What was *he* doing in Mule Hollow? He continued to glare, waiting for her answer, and she gave her brain a mental thump. After all, she'd seen plenty of cowboys before. Mule Hollow was overloaded with them.

But this was *Brent Stockwell.*

Two years ago this cowboy had been a top-ranked bronc rider, on the verge of winning the world championship, when he'd suddenly dropped out of the competition and disappeared. Not that she followed the pro rodeo circuit that closely back then, but you didn't have to in order to know Brent's face. It had been on the cover of plenty of magazines— tabloids more than anything. None of that explained what he was doing here. Or why he was wearing that scowl and poking his nose into her business.

"I'm tending my horses, cowboy," she drawled and gave him the once-over, her eyes flashing green daring him to get any closer. "The question is, what are you doing?"

"*Your* horses." Clearly baffled, he stepped back, looking around. "I thought this was Pace Gentry's place."

"Well, actually it is. I'm watching it for him." Maybe he was a friend of Pace's since they were both bronc riders.

His eyes flickered over her with doubt. "*You're* watching the place?"

"What's with the twenty questions? Yes," she said, patience wearing thin. "I'm watching the place while Pace and Sheri are out of town."

"I see." He jerked his head toward the road. "And those are the horses delivered by that rig I just met at the end of the lane?" he asked.

"How did you know that?" Now *her* confusion was growing.

"Because Pace told me they were coming this afternoon."

"Pace told you?" The statement came out flat as her stomach began to churn.

He crossed his muscled arms. "That's right. I'm here to train those horses, and I'll tell you straight out I don't want you inside that corral again. They could have trampled you."

"Whoa, wait just a minute, Mr. *Stockwell*."

She yanked her gaze away from his corded forearms. "Sheri didn't say anything to me about this."

"You know me?"

"You're kidding, right?" she asked, and couldn't help thinking the man was better-looking than his pictures—even with the scowl. "Of course I know you. But let's get back to the 'I'm-here-to-train-them' part."

The two lines between his brows deepened like plow rows. "And you are?"

"Tacy Jones," she said, feeling her brows doing some plowing of their own as she scowled back at him.

"Well, then, Tacy Jones, I'll take that," he said, reaching for the feed bucket.

Oh, no, he did not just try to horn in on her! She yanked the bucket behind her and locked her defiant emerald eyes on his. "Hold on just a doggone minute, buster. You can't just waltz in here and think I'm handing things over to you just like that. I don't care who you are, I'm watching this place until someone tells me differently—" she tossed her red hair and placed a warning finger to his hard chest "—and you can just back off." Okay, maybe now she was overreacting—*who wouldn't?*

He was really stepping on her toes. With experience derived from handling four older brothers, she gave his chest one more poke. "Something just isn't right about this."

He dropped his chin and stared at her finger for a second before lifting cool eyes to hers. "I don't know exactly what's going on here. I can, however, assure you that I'm here to train those horses and *you* had better not be climbing back in there with them again." He wrapped his hand around her finger and pulled her hand away from his chest.

His eyes were not unkind, just firm as they held hers. Standing so near him and feeling his strong hand around her own sort of made a gal crumble.

Not!

Tacy swallowed hard and yanked her hand out of his. She was the girl who got the better of cowboys and enjoyed every minute of it. She was not one to let a cowboy get the better of her. She needed to switch her approach, get things going her way, throw him off balance a bit.

"You know, I think maybe you'd better get Pace or Sheri on the phone or I might have to call the sheriff, Mr. Stockwell."

His eyes widened in disbelief. "The *sheriff?* But you know me."

"Wrong. I know who you are. But I don't know for sure what you're doing here."

"You know I'm not some horse thief come to steal Pace's horses."

"Maybe not, but you're going to have to get them on the phone and give me some proof." She gave him a bright smile…the kind she knew said, I'm smiling, but I mean business.

Brent scrubbed his jaw and his eyes narrowed. "You're a regular pain in the—"

"Whoa, watch it there, cowboy. We've got a pregnant woman in the house." *Oh yes, this could be fun.*

"You're pregnant?" he practically gasped— which Tacy thought was pretty funny.

"Not me, you ninny. Birdy." She pointed to the dog, who was more than happy to flip over and show the world that she was with pup—puppies to be exact. "But even if she wasn't, you still need to watch your mouth. It might surprise you to find out that I have been called a lady a time or two—"

His hard gaze suddenly softened and he laughed—hard—just the reaction Tacy was after. Her insides flipping over in response was the unexpected part.

"I wasn't going to say anything ugly," he said. "I was going to say you were a regular pain in the neck."

"Yeah, you forget I know who you are, Brent Stockwell. The guy I read about in the papers is no Boy Scout." A fact she'd do well to remember.

He planted his feet shoulder-width apart and stared at her with eyes gone dark and hard. "I can assure you that guy you read about has died. He's gone. So, though I'm not kidding when I tell you to stay out of that pen over there, I can assure you I wasn't about to say something out of line."

For the first time in a very long time, Tacy was speechless. What did the cowboy mean by saying he'd died? What kind of statement was that? The fact that he delivered it with such sincerity overrode everything else, yet here he was in front of her, clearly alive.

"Okay," she said, choosing to move through the awkward moment with a bit of brash humor. "I didn't mean to ruffle your feathers." What else could she say? Really?

His lip twitched. "Consider my feathers unruffled."

Not one to lose her head or her good sense, Tacy decided she'd better pull back and reevaluate this situation. She needed to make a phone call.

"Gotta go," she said as she spun away and trotted to her truck—she let Birdy have freedom between the stables and the house, so she didn't worry about leaving her behind. Besides, the dog had been staring at the cowboy like he was the best thing since kibble! *The little traitor.* But then again, she couldn't help glancing out her side window as she pulled away. Brent had pushed his hat back and was watching her with a baffled expression. Her stomach tickled looking at his classic cowboy stance: legs planted, one thumb hooked in his belt, head cocked just slightly. This wasn't over by a long shot.

Brent watched the fiery Tacy Jones drive away. With that red hair and those saucy green eyes, the woman promised to be a thorn in his side.

He'd almost had a heart attack when he'd driven up and saw her heading into the pen with those horses. Though Pace had told him they were halter-broke, that didn't make him any more pleased to see her in the middle of a bunch of unpredictable horses. Pace had a reputation for taking stubborn stock with promise and turning them around. The crazy woman could have gotten herself hurt. That she didn't act like she understood that fact was the problem.

Looking down at her dog—Birdy she'd called it—Brent gave the blue-heeler another pat on the head. The dog had to be due within the next few weeks, but that didn't keep her from dancing around, looking for attention. As he walked over to inspect the horses, she raced out ahead of him. At the corral she skidded to a halt, then placed her chin on the bottom rung of the pen and watched the horses with expectant eyes. He had a feeling she was good at her job when she wasn't carrying babies.

The colts were skittish—as expected after a long ride in a trailer. He could tell right off, though, that one of them, a pretty chestnut, had a wild look in its eyes that meant trouble. "It's always the redheads," he said, glancing at the dog. Birdy lifted her blue eyes toward him and he could have sworn she grinned. Normally he'd have laughed—not this time. He planned to have a conversation with Pace about this surprising turn of events.

Pace knew Brent's story. He certainly knew that Brent wouldn't feel comfortable with a woman hanging around the corral while he was breaking these colts. So what was going on? If Pace had brought Tacy in to watch over the place, why hadn't he warned him? He had to know seeing her would remind Brent of his sister's accident. And Brent didn't like reminders of what his stupidity and carelessness had cost Tina.

His gut hurt, remembering that moment two years before.... It had only been by the grace of God that Tina had lived—it was yet to be seen if she'd ever fully recover.

Pace knew this. Temper flaring, Brent stalked toward the cabin at the side of the property. He'd been warned that Mule Hollow's cell-phone service was practically nonexistent and he'd have to rely on the landline in the cabin to get hold of Pace. Something just didn't feel right about this entire setup. There was trouble brewing. Maybe Pace hadn't seen that look in the cowgirl's eyes…the one that said she wasn't going to let some cowboy tell her what to do.

He rubbed the spot where she'd jabbed her finger in his chest. The woman obviously thought she was going to get to train those colts, not just "look after the place." Only thing was, while he was around, there was no way *that* was happening. Absolutely no way.

Chapter Two

"What can I get you boys?" Tacy asked the booth full of cowboys who were looking up at her like expectant puppies. They acted like they'd never seen a woman taking their lunch order before. It had been this way for the two weeks since she'd taken this job at Sam's diner.

"How about a date?" Jess Tomlin drawled, giving her a wink. The same wink he'd been giving her ever since he'd first seen her behind the counter.

She pulled her order pad from her pocket. "You got somethin' in your eye?" she asked, giving him a pointed stare and holding her pencil at the ready—not that she was going to need it. It was Tuesday and Sam cooked enchiladas on Tuesday.

"C'mon, Tacy, forget him and come out with me," his buddy Chad said, sitting up straight and giving her a cocky grin.

"*Fellas*— Order?" she tapped her pad with her pencil.

"Aw, c'mon, Tacy, give a guy some hope."

"Jess, you don't need hope from me and you know it. Now either you dudes order or I'll do it for you."

The foursome grinned just as she'd expected they would and also ordered exactly what she knew they would order.

"Four specials," she called a few seconds later, hustling into the kitchen. Sam was in the midst of flipping a row of burgers. As soon as he heard the order, he reached for plates on the side shelf with his free hand and continued flipping patties with his right hand. He never skipped a beat. Tacy watched him in amazement as he used the spatula to send the meat patty into the air in a quick, tight arc. Immediately, he moved to the next patty and had it in the air before the other patty had finished its flip. Once they were all turned and dusted with salt and pepper, he reached for the ladle in the large pot on the stove. In his sixties and built like a jockey, Sam was king of his domain—a short-order cook in more ways than one.

During the lunch rush, he worked with the energy of three men. Though he had a cook who came in some evenings and a college student who also helped out evenings and Saturdays, he took very little time off.

"How in the world did you run this place before hiring help?"

Sam gave her a quick grin, dipping beans into the plates. "Didn't used ta be this busy. Used ta be a dead little town and I had it all under control. Weren't much more work than if I had folks comin' by the house fer a meal and a visit. I ain't complainin', though," he said, starting to dish up the enchiladas. "Needin' help is a good thang. I'm glad you came along when ya did."

"I'm glad you had an opening," she said, and meant it. They worked well together. She picked up the four plates, inhaling the spicy scent. "Back for the burgers in a jiffy." She gave him an affectionate smile as she headed for the dining room. She hadn't been here long, but she felt right at home. For a gal who'd been a little homesick at times, this was a very nice feeling.

As she walked back into the dining area, Tacy's spirits were high—despite her run-in with that insufferable cowboy the day before. "Here we go, boys. Chow's up!" She got a real kick out of the way the cowboys jerked to attention as she set their meal in front of them. Guys—you had to love 'em.

She really was glad to be here—true, she'd have been happier if things had worked out the way she'd planned. Housesitting, waiting tables and fending off good-natured cowboys was fun enough. Still, she'd rather be learning how to tame a horse.

She didn't hold her situation against anyone, though. Especially the thick-skulled cowboys. If they wanted to spoon it out, she could sure dish it right back at them. It was all in good fun from most of the men who frequented the place. Fellas like Jess were a different story. She knew he really did hope she'd go out with him sooner or later. That wasn't happening. Not yet. Dating wasn't in the long-range plans of her life right now. Love got in the way of plans…and this girl had plans that *nothing* was sidetracking—well, nothing except Brent Stockwell, at the moment.

All it had taken was a quick call to Sheri,

and the truth came out. Pace had called Brent and, just like that, the man had headed to Mule Hollow to take over the job that was supposed to have been hers. Feeling her neck muscles seizing up, Tacy tried hard to concentrate on her job instead of the cocky cowboy who was now her biggest obstacle. She knew Sheri had known she wouldn't be happy, and that had to be her reason for keeping silent. Grabbing the plates of hamburgers Sam had ready, Tacy headed back toward the dining room. She would not let her temper flare out of control. Despite her newfound resolve, Tacy almost dropped her armload of burgers as Brent Stockwell walked in through the heavy swinging door.

"Heads up," she drawled to the table of cowboys, proud that she was managing some semblance of calm. She slapped the plates in front of the cowboys as she kept one eye pinned on Brent. He sauntered toward the food counter and slid onto the cowhide stool. Catching her off guard he glanced around and caught her staring…okay, gawking! Now *that* was a cowboy!

Feet dragging, she went to do her job. "Hi," she said, grabbing a menu from behind the counter and setting it in front of him. "Welcome to Sam's—" she didn't call him by name; it was not her business to announce to the world who he was. She was just here to take his order "—where everyone and anyone is welcome," she added just for kicks.

He took the menu, leaned slightly forward and smiled at her. "Thanks for the welcome."

He kept his voice low and smooth so only she could hear him, as if they were sitting in a five-star restaurant with candles aglowing. "What's good?"

At sound of his voice, Tacy's mouth went dry. It was humiliating. "Everything, depending on what you feel like," she said, holding her voice steady. Thankfully her quick-witted humor came roaring to her rescue. "Sam's got a mean burger, a tough chicken-fried steak and the enchiladas are to die for—and that's just for starters. The meat loaf is a real kick in the pants, too."

He gave her a lopsided grin that added insult to injury. "Sounds like my kind of food," he drawled.

"Best in Texas," she drawled right back at him. "Quesadillas are killer, too, but you don't strike me as the quesadilla type."

His clear turquoise eyes twinkled in challenge. "You'd be right about that." He laid the menu down and cupped his hands on the counter, his gaze never wavering from hers.

"Yep. Not nearly macho enough." She crinkled her nose in teasing distaste. "Quesadillas are for *girls*."

His lip curled into a slow smile. "Something like that," he said as the smile reached his eyes.

No wonder he'd been such a ladies' man back when he was making headlines. "So what'll it be?" she asked, fighting to keep her wits about her. The day before, the man had treated her like she was an idiot who couldn't be trusted around horses. Today he was flirting with her—and she was enjoying it, no matter how much she didn't want to.

"Why don't you pick for me," he said, interrupting her internal commotion. "You know what I don't like. See if you can guess what I do like."

Huffing like he was getting on her last nerve—*because he really was, in more ways than one*—she tapped her pencil on the pad and met his teasing challenge. "Are we talking the whole menu or just the items I've told you about so far?"

He grinned. "The items you've told me about so far."

"Too easy, but here goes. I'd say that on occasion you enjoy a good chicken-fried steak, smothered with gravy and saddled up with a heaping order of mashed potatoes—" He started to say something and she held up her hand. "Not so fast, buster. I'm not done. I said *on occasion* that's what you enjoy. But this afternoon I'm going with the meat loaf."

He looked genuinely surprised. "And how exactly did you figure that out?"

She shook her head. "Sorry, a girl doesn't reveal her secrets." She walked to the kitchen. "One meat loaf, Sam. Light on the gravy," she called through the swinging café doors.

"Comin' right up," Sam fired back, glancing her way and lifting a questioning brow. "You shor—"

"That's what the cowboy ordered," she shot back.

"Well, alrighty then. One meat loaf comin' right up. You seen what time it is?"

"Yes, I hate to leave you, though."

"Rush hour's done. I got it from here and my Adela is expecting you."

"Okay. I'll get the meat loafer's drink and then catch you tomorrow."

"Got it, kiddo."

She spun back to Brent, more than ready to leave. "What'll you have to drink? Tea, soda, coffee?"

"You're so good at this, what do you think the, ah, *meat loafer* wants?"

"Nope again. I'm not choosing your drink for you. I'm one for one and my shift's over so I don't want to chance ruining my perfect score."

"In that case, I'll take a tall glass of iced tea."

She grabbed a glass and filled it with ice, then reached for the pitcher. "You get the horses settled?" she asked, her curiosity getting the better of her even as she glanced at the clock.

"Pretty much. You talk to Sheri?"

She placed his tea in front of him. "Yup. Seems they just forgot to tell me you were filling in. Looks like I'm not going to get to call the law on you after all." *Doggoneit!*

"You mean I'm going to get to stick around and do my job?"

She snorted. "Not by my choice." She ignored the fact that her traitor pulse did a little yee-haw at the idea of him sticking around Mule Hollow.

"I'm just doing what Pace asked me to do. And whether you want to believe it or not, it's for the best."

"Well, isn't that just peachy," she gritted through a fake smile. "This has been real fun but I've gotta run." Boy, did she. "Sam will take *real* good care of you, though." At the end of the counter she paused. "And remember, I warned you about the meat loaf."

"Warned me?" His straight brows dipped questioningly.

"Yup." She arched a brow, grabbed her purse from under the counter and headed toward the door.

She grinned all the way out to her truck. Poor dude should have had the quesadillas.

Brent watched Tacy sashay out of the building to the catcalls from several tables of cowboys. Her vibrant, copper-colored hair was pulled back into a ponytail and danced a jig as she plowed through the diner, waving goodbye to the room on her way out the door. He had to admit she was cute. No doubt about it—and obviously popular. Not that he was interested.

He had no intention of pursuing any kind of relationship while he was here. He didn't want to do anything that had the potential to keep him in this town. He was here to do a job for his buddy, Pace, and then he was out of here—back to getting his life back on track… maybe back to the circuit and a dream he'd wasted.

"So yor the brave one?" a short, weathered man said as he busted through the swinging café doors from the kitchen. He was holding a steaming plate of meat loaf and beans that he plopped onto the bar in front of Brent.

"The brave one?" Brent repeated, and had the feeling Tacy had neglected to tell him something important.

"Yup. It's not ever'body that can stomach my meat loaf. It's a real kick in the pants. It ain't fer girls and that's fer shor—if you know what I mean."

"Oh, yeah," Brent drawled, suddenly pretty sure he got the whole picture. He grinned. "How about handing me that hot sauce I see back behind you there."

That got him a big grin and an extended palm. "I'm Sam, and you sound like a cowboy I can admire."

Brent shook Sam's hand—and as the tiny man took hold of his hand, Brent felt like he'd just stuck his fingers in a vise grip.

"Brent Stockwell. Glad to make your acquaintance, sir," he gritted out as normal-sounding as he could manage, seeing as how his hand was in a world of hurt.

Sam released him at last and reached for the hot sauce. "You ain't bit into that meat loaf yet. You might be ready fer a fight come thirty minutes."

Brent laughed. "I'm sure it's not that bad." He took a bite, chewed and got the kick of peppers. He'd tasted hotter. This was all good. "Tacy wasn't lying when she said this was good."

Sam's eyes widened. "She said that, did she?"

Brent nodded. Pretty certain she'd said it—then again, maybe not in so many words. He took another bite. Sam watched, wiry arms crossed over his chest.

"Brent Stockwell. That thar name sounds mighty familiar."

Brent didn't say anything, just kept on eating. He really didn't think his past would make any difference to the older man. In this part of Texas, there were plenty of cowboys with just as many buckles as he had.

"World-class bronc buster—I remember now," Sam drawled. "So what brings you ta Mule Hollow?"

And that was that, Brent thought with relief. This might be okay after all. Pace had assured him he'd blend in and be just another cowboy in this neck of the woods. "I'm here to break and train horses for Pace Gentry."

"Fer *Pace?*"

Brent nodded, starting to feel the heat of the peppers. "Yeah, he called and said he was in a bind and wondered if I could help him out for a couple of months."

"Tacy know about this? Know about you?"

Brent noticed Sam looking a bit baffled. "We met yesterday when I arrived. Is something wrong?"

"No. I'm jest surprised 'cause she didn't say nothin'. I ain't heard about this 'til now."

Brent took another bite of the meat loaf. His tongue was burning now, and he decided maybe he wouldn't add any hot sauce. He took a swig of tea. Coughed and took another swig of tea. His eyes watered slightly. He took another swig and thought he had it under control until a cough ambushed him. The meat loaf was good but smokin', and that was going easy on the fire it was packing. "It was kinda spur-of-the-moment, I think. He realized he was going to be tied up longer than he planned and he had fresh horses comin' in that needed takin' care of." He ended with a cough.

Sam nodded and grinned. "Well, I think that's gonna be a real fine situation. Still want this hot sauce?"

"No, sir, I think I'm good."

"Yup, ain't nobody ever needed to add spice to my meat loaf. I'm surprised yor still eatin'."

Brent felt like his throat was starting to close up. "I can understand that, sir." He bit back a cough and drained his glass of tea. Sam picked up the pitcher and held it up, offering a refill. Brent held out his glass and was tempted to grab the pitcher and down it as the peppers kicked in full force!

Tacy was probably laughing her pretty head off at the joke she'd just pulled on him. When he got through dying, he'd probably think it was funny, too…maybe.

* * *

She really should be ashamed of herself, Tacy thought as she left the diner and headed out to Pace's place to take Rabbit, her own horse, out for some exercise. She should feel bad—but she didn't. Sam insisted on fixing that meat loaf every morning and every night he threw most of it away. Not even the buzzards would touch the stuff. But he did it because he said when cowboys needed to challenge each other to some sort of wager—which a cowboy just couldn't help doing on a regular basis—his meat loaf was the perfect thing. The loser got to eat it! He kept it on hand for just such occasions, and he got a real kick out of watching the cowboys sweat bullets while downing the hot stuff.

Tacy knew to warn new customers away from it, but Brent Stockwell had just been too tempting. Still, as upset as she was with the guy, there was something about him that she was overwhelmingly drawn to.... Her and every other woman on the planet! From what she'd seen on the covers of all those tabloids, he'd escorted a parade of different women on his arm. Watching his love life two years ago had been a national pastime. It would only be a matter of time before someone other than Tacy realized who Brent was. And then what?

She would be curious to see how Mule Hollow would handle having a celebrity in its midst.

The thing was—why did she care? She might be a little curious as to why he'd disappeared from the circuit two years before when he had been on such a roll. No, she cared because he was here to take her job away, that's why. No curiosity about his past and no butterflies-in-the-stomach, adolescent infatuation with the man was going to change that fact. The only thing about Brent that interested her was how to get him to rethink his stand on her being around those horses. Maybe he would if he forgave her for the meat loaf first!

Chapter Three

"Birdy!" Tacy scolded the next morning after she stumbled over something that shouldn't have been in her path and dropped her travel cup of coffee on the porch. A quick glance down revealed a boot, a cowboy's riding boot with the spur still strapped on. "Bad dog," she mumbled as her gaze fell on Birdy, who was flopped on her stomach with her chin on her paws, eyes watching Tacy expectantly.

"You have done a bad thing, young lady," she said, bending to retrieve her cup and the boot. Striding to her truck, she dropped the boot in the back and gave Birdy another stern look. "You're gonna get me in trouble if you start stealing our neighbors' boots. You don't mess with a man's boots." Birdy cocked her head and didn't look the least bit repentant. "I'm serious—no stealing." Birdy barked once and wiggled her tail, totally ignoring Tacy's scowl as she lowered the tailgate. "I am such a sucker. Hop in." Birdy sprang into the back, spun and licked Tacy on the cheek.

"Yeah, yeah, I love you, too."

She knew the boot had to be Brent's, and after yesterday's meat-loaf incident, she wasn't looking forward to returning it.

The man just plain disturbed her, and he was taking up too much of her thoughts. Aside from the fact that she found him—the bad boy of the rodeo circuit—disturbingly attractive, there were the things he'd said when they first met—that he'd died—that kept coming back to her. What had he meant?

Two years ago he'd been such a party-hearty cowboy that it was amazing the man had time to stay on the top of the rodeo leaderboard.

Then he'd disappeared because of a rumored family emergency. He'd dropped out of competition, and off the front covers of the tabloids. He was just gone.

Now he was back—in Mule Hollow—and taking over her job. She could understand Sheri and Pace's explanation. They'd had to bring Brent in because they weren't going to be back in time to honor their contract. The horses were contracted to have sixty days' riding on them before they were picked up at the end of December. Since Pace wasn't going to be there to do it, he'd called in the next best thing—Brent. Those were Sheri's words.

Sheri had told Tacy to talk Brent into letting her help him. Yeah, right. As badly as she wanted to learn to break horses, she wasn't the kind of gal who begged anyone for anything. Then again, she wasn't the kind of gal who let a guy tell her what she could and could not do, either. Maybe that had been part of the reason she'd conned him into eating that meat loaf the day before. Who knew? She'd taken Rabbit out for some exercise in the pasture when she got home from the café and half expected him to be waiting for her when she rode back to the barn. But he hadn't been around. If he couldn't tolerate hot stuff, that meat loaf probably burned a hole in his stomach.

Maybe he liked it hot, because now he was striding out of the barn as she parked the truck.

"Hey, cowboy," she called, climbing out of the cab and walking with his boot extended in front of her. "I bring a peace offering," she said handing him his boot.

"This is my boot."

"Very good. That is, in fact, *your* boot," she said. To her surprise, Brent chuckled.

"This is your peace offering? My own boot?"

"You don't like it?"

"I like it a lot. Thanks."

She grinned. "You're very welcome," she said, striding past him and heading toward Rabbit's stall. "Hey, boy," she cooed as she lifted the latch and entered. Brent had followed her into the barn and was now leaning against the gate, watching her. Her pulse started doing that erratic drumbeat that did not make her happy at all.

"So why are you so adamantly against my getting in that pen with those horses?" Tacy had decided to just cut straight to the problem. "I came here to learn to train horses, and now you're standing in my way. Is it something personal?"

"You're not one to mince words, are you?" he said, startled.

"No, I'm not. And you're not a chauvinist, so what's the problem?"

A grin spread across his handsome face.

She looked at the horse blanket she was settling on Rabbit's back, feeling Brent's gaze on her.

"What makes you think I'm not just a male chauvinist who doesn't want a woman out there?"

"Not your style." She walked past him to retrieve her saddle from its stand.

He crossed his arms and watched as she hefted the saddle. "You like to think you can read people, don't you?"

She paused, grinning. "Bad habit I have."

"So how did you know I liked meat loaf?"

She grimaced. "How do you know that wasn't just a lucky guess?"

She started to walk past him, halting when he moved slightly in front of her.

"That was no guess."

She swallowed, not expecting to find herself so close to him. "Okay," she said, sidestepping around him as her pulse careened. "So I remembered reading once that meat loaf was your favorite food."

He followed her into the stall, and she could feel him close beside her as she placed the saddle on Rabbit's back. She was so embarrassed—it wasn't as if she read those magazines. Well, she had read the covers, and she did admit that sometimes when she found herself standing in line she'd scanned them, looking specifically for his name.

"You read stories in the tabloids about me?"

She spun toward him. "Why would you say that? You were at the top of your game when you were riding. You were written up in more than just the gossip rags." Drat. She'd just admitted how much she had followed the cowboy.

"You didn't exactly strike me as the type to read that trash." He strode out of the barn and she followed him. His sarcasm and stiff posture told her that he was really angry. Tacy suddenly had the overwhelming need to justify herself. "I didn't read them. I *did* read an article about you in the *Horseman,* though," she said. "I really and truly never flipped through those other magazines. I'm a grocery store headline reader, that's all."

He stopped between the barn and the corral. "Most of that stuff wasn't true. It's pure fantasy."

"However, inquiring minds sometimes can't help reading them." Her comment made him scowl. "Sorry, I was just teasing," she said.

His gaze looked tortured as he lifted his rope from the fence and tightened the coil. She almost let it go. Almost. There was something about the way he looked standing there tense as a fence post and as hard as a block of ice.

Don't butt in, the voice in her head hollered. But she forged ahead. "So you're going to enlighten me about the truth, right?" The soft snorting of the horses that were moving about on the other side of the fence sounded loud in the tense silence as he lifted his gaze to hers.

"No, I'm not. As soon as I hit the circuit again, nosy reporters will try to expose my life like an open book, and I don't know what kind of lies and twists will be attached. I'd rather not think about all that now." His tone softened a bit and his accusing gaze gave way to one that almost begged her to understand.

Tacy's curiosity skyrocketed, but she only gave a light nod. After all, it was his business. Still, when Brent spun on his heel and strode into the horse pen, she couldn't take her eyes off him. What had happened to him?

Tacy stood there for the longest time as Brent worked the rope. His back and shoulders barely moved as the rope twirled above his head. With a quick flick, he let the loop fly toward the group of horses, and there was no mistaking which horse he had in his sights. Nor was there a question in her mind about whether the loop would land easily around the horse's neck.

Brent Stockwell was poetry in motion. Cowboy poetry. And as the horse he chose reared, hooves pawing the air, head twisting from side to side, Brent took up the slack on the rope and walked calmly toward the uncertain animal, reeling it in with no fear.

As he talked gently to the horse, Tacy watched the animal fall under his influence. Tacy was afraid she was doing exactly the same thing. Only she wasn't going to let herself back down and give up her dream. Oh, no, she was going to break horses, with or without his help.

She'd be lying to herself if she said she wasn't intrigued by Brent. She was…but that didn't matter. Her main goal was to figure out how to get Brent to teach her to do what he just did. Before she could tame horses, she was going to have to tame the man!

Chapter Four

On his third morning in Mule Hollow, Brent hopped in his truck at twenty to six and headed to Sam's for an early-morning breakfast. He glanced at Pace's house as he passed it, and couldn't help but think of the feisty redhead probably still sleeping inside.

He had not planned on Tacy when he'd agreed to take this job. The fact that she knew about him—or thought she did—bothered him. It wasn't as if he was that famous or anything. His picture had been on the front page of those tabloids two years ago.... Thankfully, hardly anyone recognized him these days. If they did, it was only because they were connected to the rodeo circuit in some way. Sam hadn't cared one way or the other. Normally, he didn't let it bother him if someone knew him and mentioned his past stupidity—dating TV stars and acting like he was somebody special. Tina's accident had sobered him up in more ways than one. Knowing Tacy had read all that trash about him—it bothered him. More than he wanted it to.

The woman was something—"Something else," he growled. A distraction he wouldn't mind as long as she stayed out of the horse pen.

When he pulled up in front of the diner, two older men were disappearing through the swinging door ahead of him.

He removed his hat as he entered, realizing they were the first patrons of the morning.

"You came back," Sam said, grinning as Brent sat down on the same stool he'd chosen the day before.

"I'm back, but—" he held up his hands "—I don't believe I'll be having the meat loaf."

The two older men had set their checkerboard on the table by the front window and come to stand at the counter. They studied him. At the mention of meat loaf, their dour looks turned into grins.

"So yor the one that ate the meat loaf?" the

thin one said loudly. "Big TV star like yourself got hoodwinked, didn't ya?"

Brent's palms dampened at the mention of the TV spots. Sam hadn't said anything about that, but Brent should have known he'd seen the commercials. Brent had snagged a few endorsements during his bid for the championship.

The other man shook his balding head. "That's not a good thang. Not good at all."

Brent didn't know if the man was referring to the meat-loaf episode or the TV spots. Brent was in agreement on both counts.

Sam chuckled and set a cup of coffee in front of Brent. "I told y'all Tacy got him. She recommended the meat loaf and didn't tell him about all the peppers I load it up with."

That got a hoot from all three of them and Brent couldn't help chuckling along with them. He was relieved that they seemed more interested in Tacy's reactions than his past. She'd definitely pulled a smooth one on him.

"So what'd ya do ta make her mad at ya?"

Brent looked at the skinny guy. "I asked her what she recommended. She said the meat loaf."

"That's Tacy. She's a root-tootin' live wire.

By the way, I'm Applegate Thornton, but you can call me App," the skinny guy said, holding out his hand.

Brent shook, glad App didn't lock on to his hand with the same grip that Sam had.

"And I'm Stanley. Stanley Orr. Glad ta make yor acquaintance. Sam said you was here ta train horses fer Pace."

"Yes, sir. That's true."

Sam had been grinning through the whole exchange. "That thar's why Tacy tricked him into eatin' the meat loaf. He surprised her out thar. Poor gal didn't have a clue you was showin' up here."

"You mean she didn't *know?*" App's eyes widened beneath bushy brows.

Sam shook his head. "Shore didn't. Pace and Sheri never said nothin'."

Stanley let out a low whistle. "She didn't get mad, did she? She got even." He and his two buddies got a good laugh out of that.

"Serious, though," Stanley said, "why would that make her mad? Yor good with horses, so you kin teach her same as Pace was goin' to. Right?"

Brent didn't want to get into this, but it couldn't be helped. "No. I won't teach her."

Three groans went up around him.

"She know that?" Stanley asked as his buddies leaned in with raised bushy brows.

"Hey," Brent said, suddenly feeling defensive. "I told her I didn't want her in the pen with the horses, and she got a little peeved. Why are y'all looking like that? It's for her own good."

"Tell him, Sam," Applegate prompted.

"She came here to learn to train them horses," Sam said. "That's the only reason Tacy's in Mule Hollow. The little spitfire wants ta not only train 'em, she wants to *break* 'em."

"Over my dead body," Brent mumbled, swallowing a big swig of coffee.

"That may be, if you get in her way," Stanley said, grabbing a handful of sunflower seeds out of a bag. "She's got her heart set on it."

App crossed his arms and assessed Brent with warning eyes. "Yup, she does, and I don't thank she's the type ta have some ole cowboy tellin' her what and *what not* she kin do."

"Even one that does foo-foo commercials," Stanley added, hiking a bushy brow and grinning wider.

"Ain't that the truth," App grunted, leaning forward to sniff the air close to Brent. "Men—

especially self-respectin' cowboys—ain't spos'd ta smell prissy."

So much for no teasing. Brent decided against pointing out that it had been two lousy cologne commercials—about which he'd been teased mercilessly by every cowboy on the circuit.

Sam chuckled, clearly enjoying Brent's discomfort before taking pity on him and reeling the conversation back in. "I jest don't see Tacy walkin' away. Pace was supposed to teach her."

App and Stanley sobered. "Yup," they said in unison.

"*Pace* agreed to that?" Brent didn't like what he was hearing.

"Well, yeah," Sam said, slapping his palms on the counter as he glared at Brent. "You ain't listening. She ain't from here. She came here just fer the reason of learnin' ta break them horses."

"Pace didn't tell me any of that. I'm sorry, fellas, but that agreement was between Tacy and Pace. My agreement with Pace has nothing to do with putting Tacy at risk. No way am I teaching a woman how to get up on the back of a bucking horse." Not after he'd helped his sister do exactly that, and he'd almost gotten her killed.

"Calm down," Stanley said, placing a hand on Brent's shoulder.

"Yeah, you don't look so good," App said, peering close. "She's a good little gal. No need ta get angry at her."

Brent picked up his coffee. "I'm not angry at her. I'm just not the guy to teach her to break a horse. She'll have to take that up with Pace when he gets back." He might have to have a word with Pace about that, too. "Sam, how about some eggs, sir?"

Sam grinned. "I'm fixin' ta cook 'em right up." He headed toward the kitchen and App and Stanley went over to their table and the checkerboard. He wasn't too sure he understood why someone would want to play checkers at the crack of dawn. To each his own—they liked checkers this early; he liked riding horses this early.

"Sam," he called. "No funny business. I had heartburn like you wouldn't believe."

All three of the men thought that was funny and hooted and chortled with laughter. Brent didn't join them, as his thoughts turned back to Tacy. He hoped she wouldn't ask him to teach her to break horses. She'd told him he was in her way and made it clear that she thought she was capable—his sister had believed the same thing, and only by the grace of God was she still alive. Brent was counting his blessings and had absolutely no intention of being part of that kind of foolishness again.

Especially with Tacy Jones. The woman was a wild card. It would be a shame to risk something happening to somebody who was obviously so full of life.

If she asked, he'd just tell her no.

There were much worse things in life than being told no.

"So I got this idea about the Thanksgiving festival," Norma Sue Jenkins said.

Tacy had just poured coffee into Norma's cup and refilled Norma's two friends' cups and couldn't help listening in on their conversation. She liked it when they came in for afternoon coffee, when the diner was quiet because the cowboys were all out working. Norma was a hoot, a robust ranching woman with a robust personality. Along with her friends, Esther Mae Wilcox and Adela Green—

Sam's wife—Norma was considered the heart of this tiny town. These three ladies loved Mule Hollow and everything about keeping it a place where people wanted to move and raise their families.

"Well, I hope it's something new," Esther Mae said, patting her red hair. "I'm getting a bit bored with the same ole festivals."

Adela, a small woman with a gentle smile and soft white hair, nodded. "Me, too. We do need something to keep visitors wanting to come back for more. What's your idea, Norma?"

"Pumpkin' chunkin'," she said, grinning so wide her smile stretched across her round face, making her look a bit like a grinning pumpkin herself. "Or 'punkin chunkin,' which is the right term for the contest."

Esther Mae gasped. "You mean, where people bring those funny contraptions and see who can shoot a pumpkin the longest distance?"

Norma nodded enthusiastically. "Yes, that's exactly what I mean. I think that would be a riot."

"Oh, I do, too!" Esther Mae exclaimed. "I saw it done on some TV show and those people had a blast coming up with those odd-looking contraptions and cannons and such."

Sam came around the counter, his interest piqued. "Some of them are huge."

"I know," Norma Sue agreed. "And I told my Roy Don that I wanted to build one myself."

That got Tacy's attention. "You know how to do that?"

Adela smiled sweetly. "Oh, our Norma Sue is a whiz at fixing things. I'm sure she could build something. Isn't that right, dear?" she said, looking up at Sam. He grinned at his wife like a schoolboy in love, and Tacy's heartstrings tugged.

"It's true. That jukebox used to be a mess until Norma Sue finally got it fixed."

Confused, Tacy glanced at the colorful old jukebox in the corner. "Wait a minute. It doesn't always play the right song."

Esther Mae harrumphed loudly and frowned as she glanced toward the machine. "Believe me. It never used to play the right song. Drove me slap crazy. Thankfully, Norma kept working on it 'til it's much better now."

"I'm gonna fix it completely one of these days," Norma said, eyeing the machine. "Fer now, I figure it has a right to have a quirk. So what do y'all think? I'm gonna shoot this idea by Lacy and the rest of the festival committee. Are y'all on board?"

"Shore, we're on board," Sam said. "I can jest hear ole App and Stanley when they find out about it. If you're gonna build a contraption, they probably will, too, jest so they kin beat you, Norma Sue."

Esther Mae harrumphed again, crossing her arms over her pink-velour-covered chest. "Them two couldn't build a rubber-band shooter that would stand up to anything Norma Sue could build."

Sam grinned. "It don't matter if they could or not. I jest have me a feelin' we might have ourselves a little competition among friends once they hear ole Norma's buildin' a machine."

Norma Sue's grin grew slowly across her face like a war flag unfurling. "If them boys want to issue me a challenge, you tell 'em ta bring it on."

Tacy laughed. Mule Hollow just got a whole lot more interesting. She'd already learned that App and Stanley loved to pick on Norma Sue and Esther Mae, and she had a feeling this was going to be fun to watch. There might even be a few fireworks.

* * *

Brent was working with a hardheaded colt when Tacy drove into the yard the next morning. He didn't look in her direction, though he was tempted. The gal had spunk. She was lean and leggy, like a colt, but there was nothing gangly about Tacy. She was quick on her feet, and he'd noticed that she was easy around her horse. There was no denying that she had a way with it.

He'd watched her ride, knew she was good. Two years ago, before his sister had been hurt, before he'd learned his lesson, he wouldn't have had any problem teaching her how to break a horse. Back then, he'd been a fool.

He could feel Tacy's eyes on his back, watching as he worked with the colt. It was a nervous colt, and building trust between himself and the horse was the most important thing about breaking it the gentle way.

"She's trusting you more today," Tacy said, her voice soft, easy.

"She's a smart one. Nervous, but smart."

"I think you'd probably say that about any gal who did what you told her to do."

She was teasing, yet she wasn't. He patted the horse on the neck and kept his mouth shut. Maybe she'd go ride Rabbit and leave him in peace.

"How long you been at it?" she asked.

The mare got spooked and spun away from him. Holding the lead rope so she couldn't get too far away, Brent turned with her and found himself looking straight at Tacy.

"A little rebellion," she said before he answered her. "I like this horse."

"You would."

"The man speaks."

He grinned. "When he wants to."

"So what time did you start?"

He looked at the mare's deep brown eyes. "Six-thirty. Why?"

"Just wondering what time I should start showing up in the mornings so I can get in on everything."

"Don't you have a horse to ride?"

"Not today." She folded her arms over the next-to-the-top bar and laid her chin on them. Her eyes sparkled.

Brent's stomach clenched looking at her.

"I'm here to watch."

He spoke gently to the horse while studying Tacy. The woman wasn't taking no for an answer…and while he admired that trait in a man or woman, he wasn't too happy about it right now.

"Well, don't just stand there—ignore me and continue what you were doing," she said, chuckling like tinkling glass.

"That's kind of hard to do with you distracting me."

"Why, Mr. Stockwell, I had no idea you felt that way about me."

He shook his head. "Cute," he grumbled as his concentration went south once and for all. He was going to have a long talk with her after he ended this session with the roan.

"You have the saddle in the pen with you. Does that mean you're about to try to put it on her?"

He pressed his hand along the horse's hip, and she moved away from the pressure just as he'd wanted her to do. Then he tossed the end of his rope across her back, and she accepted it with only a few twitches of her ears and a little flinch. He'd been working with the mare for two days to get her accustomed to him and the rope. Today he was moving up to the saddle blanket and then the saddle. Tomorrow he'd ride her. He didn't tell Tacy any of this. It sounded easy—and actually it was, once you knew what you were doing. But that didn't take the margin for error out of the equation.

To his surprise, Tacy didn't ask any more questions. She watched. He glanced at her from beneath his Stetson and didn't miss that she was drinking in his every move with those alert green eyes of hers. She winked when she caught him staring, but said nothing.

He moved to the fence and picked up the saddle blanket. While he was holding the lead rope, he settled the blanket on the horse's back. She took it fairly well. "Good girl," he murmured, lifting it up several times and letting it fall back down. Each time, she accepted it without trying to run. Her trust was growing. After a few more minutes, Brent reached for the saddle.

Chapter Five

Tacy had been surprised that Brent hadn't pitched a fit about her hovering. Good. She knew she was pushing her welcome, but she couldn't help that. She'd come out the day before and *forced* herself to stride right past the pen where he was working. She'd saddled Rabbit and gone about her business before heading home to get ready for work. Not today. She just hadn't been able to do it. She figured if she got him used to her being around, eventually he'd give in. Kind of like the way he broke a horse. The thought made her smile as she watched him building trust with the roan. Really, what was he so worried about? She could do what he was doing. No problem. Watching him made her more confident than ever. If there was one thing Tacy didn't lack it was confidence. She knew she would be a good trainer once she was given the chance.

When Brent went for the saddle, she held her breath. She wanted to ask questions, but held back.

He'd gotten the horse somewhat used to the blanket and was now talking softly and using clicking noises to take his relationship to the next level. One-handed—something she would never be able to do—he placed the saddle on the horse's back. It barely moved.

No bucking, no hop and skip. Nothing. Its nostrils flared and its ears twitched, yet the animal stood there with only those big velvet eyes shifting as she looked at Brent. Yep, no doubt about it, the man knew what he was doing. And he made it look easy. She'd seen her brothers working with a troublesome horse before and it never went this smoothly.

She watched him for another hour as he patiently got the horse used to the saddle and the cinches. Keeping her mouth closed and not asking questions was one of the hardest things she'd ever done.

When he finally turned the roan out into

the large pen and came striding out of the round pen carrying the saddle and blanket, she fell into step beside him.

"That was really awesome. I've never seen a horse go so willingly from green to saddle-ready."

He stopped, flung the saddle onto its wooden rest just inside the barn entrance and tossed the blanket onto the fence, then turned quickly toward her. This movement brought them so close Tacy had to back up a step to stare up at him. It felt as if they were squaring off for a fight. She realized with one look into those stormy eyes of his that this was a fair assessment of the situation.

"I'm not playing this game with you," he bit out, his calm trust-me tone gone.

"What game?" Might as well make him real mad—she was getting there herself. The man was really something when he was about to blow.

"You know exactly what I'm talking about," he ground out, meeting her gaze with steely eyes.

She kept her cool. "I was just admiring your technique."

His jaw clenched and she had a sudden

urge to place her hand against it. That was not happening. Touching Brent Stockwell wouldn't be a smart move.

"You're having fun, aren't you?" The question was low, resembling Clint Eastwood's "Make my day."

"Maybe," she murmured, her pulse strumming like white-water rapids. She could see the danger signs, hear alarm bells chiming. Did that stop her? Oh, no, the thrill of the ride was too tempting—not to mention that she really hated being told no. She smiled. "Surely you didn't expect me just to give up."

"Yeah, I did." His shoulders stiffened, bringing his chest closer to her. "If you know what's good for you, you'd better listen up." His breath feathered across her skin like warm honey on toast.

Tacy's comeback lodged in her throat. They stared at each other, her gaze drifting to the grim lines of his lips. This was not good. Her thoughts broke as he suddenly spun away and stalked to the barn door. Slamming his hand to the rough wood, he stared out toward the cabin, every line of his body tense as the sun silhouetted him in an orange spotlight. Dust and floating hay specks played in the shaft of light, making a hazy halo around him—yet doing little to soften the tension radiating from him.

She was breathless. She hadn't experienced such a maddening attraction…well, ever. But this wasn't just attraction; it was an intense game of wills and she was mad. The cowboy was demanding that she do as he said. *And* calling her dumb if she didn't do it…ha! She strode past him into the sunlight and paused to look over her shoulder. "Just so you know, I don't like being told what to do. And unless you're going to figure out a way to lock me off the property, you're stuck with me, cowboy."

He was clearly unhappy, but she was too mad to care as she headed to her truck. "You have a good day," Tacy tossed over her shoulder before climbing into the cab and then driving off.

It was a wonder she could see the road for all the steam clouding her eyes.

"Mom, I've committed to getting these horses ready." Brent had been so mad he couldn't think straight after Tacy left. He'd come inside the cabin for a glass of water when the phone rang. He'd been dreading another conversation with his mom about why he wasn't coming home for Thanksgiving. The truth was, he wasn't ready....

"Brent. We miss you. And Thanksgiving just isn't the same without you here to share it with us. Tina really wants you to come home. She's doing well—"

"Mom, if I come home it will just be more reminders of what I've cost her. You know Dad doesn't want me back there. And with good reason."

"Brent, your father is a hard man, but he's a good man. He misses you."

His gaze fell to the floor and he blinked hard, feeling his father's disappointment to the core of his soul. His father had taught him almost everything he knew. All Jonas Stockwell had ever wanted was for his son to be a responsible man. For months before the tragedy, he'd been telling Brent that he was letting success go to his head. Warned him, over and over again, that a real man didn't take a God-given talent like Brent's and risk throwing it away as he was doing. How many times had he told Brent that he'd started losing sight of his goals?

He'd been right. Only it had been Tina who'd lost because Brent had been too drunk and too cocky to tell her no. To tell her it was too dangerous for her to get on the troubled colt he'd brought home to break. His sister was a bit hardheaded and hadn't wanted to listen to him. In the end, because the alcohol had affected his good sense and because he was too full of himself, not only had he let her get on that horse, but he'd helped her. His dad hadn't been able to forgive him for that.

Brent completely understood. He would never forgive himself.

"Mom, it's best if I don't come home."

A few minutes later, after a few more protests, he told his mom goodbye and walked out to the porch. Thanksgiving was three weeks away. As far as he was concerned, it might as well not even be on the calendar. Until the day Tina was one hundred percent healed, he couldn't feel any kind of thanksgiving in his heart.

He was here, back from the wilds of Idaho, simply because Pace had pointed out that Brent had to step up and stop hiding. Even if he couldn't forgive himself, he could gain some semblance of his self-respect back. He owed his dad that much. Taking Pace's job offer, training these horses, getting his life back on track…that might be a way to at least show his dad that he'd learned from his mistakes. In his dad's eyes, a man took responsibility for his mistakes and he fixed them. Brent agreed. But he couldn't fix Tina. All he could do now was try to make something of his life again. Until then, he couldn't look his dad in the eye.

He took a steady breath of the crisp November air and studied Birdy. She'd opted to stay behind and was now sprawled on the top step, looking up at him. She was a reminder that Tacy would be back soon, pushing his buttons again. Cute spitfire that she was, she had no idea what she was asking of him. No idea that her requests were something that would never happen as long as he was overseeing these horses.

"No, that ain't gonna work," Applegate said, staring at the paper on the table by the window.

Stanley glared at him. "It will, you old coot."

Tacy had been shocked when she got to work and found App and Stanley sitting at their table without a checkerboard between them. Instead, they had pencils and paper. One glance showed rough drawings of all sorts of contraptions. "Let me guess, you fellas are building a pumpkin chunker."

"They wish," Norma Sue called from a booth on the other side of the room.

"Not wish—we're doin' it," Stanley said, grabbing the pages and stacking them neatly. "It seems we got ourselves a competition going on here."

"Yup," Applegate said, giving Norma Sue a scowl.

Tacy had been in a foul mood when she'd walked in the door, still hot under the collar about her new neighbor—Mr. Official-Thorn-in-Her-Side Stockwell. Even so, seeing the spark of challenge in the room made her smile and she couldn't refrain from teasing. "Is it true what they say about Norma Sue being a whiz with anything mechanical?"

Stanley coughed as App snorted, "I ain't no slouch myself. She kin fix toasters…I kin fix oil rigs. Did it fer years."

Stanley grinned. "That's right. So it looks like we gonna have ourselves a real fine competition goin' on."

Jess Tomlin was sitting at the table across

from App and Stanley, giving Tacy his never-ending looks. She'd been too preoccupied with thoughts of Brent to even begin their normal banter. Now he jumped into the fray. "Y'all do know that punkin chunkin is serious business for some folks. They spend all year working on their machines."

Norma Sue chuckled. "We're not having a world championship chunkin contest. We're just having a friendly little beginners' contest. No pumpkin cannons or anything like that. I saw one where they were almost able to shoot a pumpkin a mile with that big cannon."

"They do it with compressed air," Applegate said, rubbing his chin.

"And it can be dangerous," Jess said. "My favorite thing to watch is the trebuchets and catapults."

"What's a trebuchet?" Tacy had to ask. She'd never have suspected that Jess would be interested in anything other than women and horses. He grinned at her.

"It's a weird contraption that has an arm that spins vertically, sending the pumpkin flying. Some folks make the arm spin by hooking up a bicycle to it. You can do the same thing with a catapult, I think."

"I saw one of them," Norma Sue said, tugging at her ear, making her kinky gray hair indent like she was poking a piece of steel wool. "It was the weirdest-looking thing." She chuckled. "I don't think we have to worry about App and Stanley riding a bike to toss their gourds."

The diner rumbled with laughter and Applegate's scowl disappeared as even he laughed along with the crowd. "Now, Norma, that is one thang y'all don't have ta anticipate seein'. It would give us all a kick, though, if you hopped on a bike and put the pedal to the metal!"

"Oh!" Esther Mae squealed. "I'd pay to see that myself." She was grinning like gangbusters until Norma Sue shot her a glare. She glared right back. "Well, I would."

"Maybe I'd pay to see you doing that, too. You're the one always hopping on that miniature trampoline of yours."

"Oh, I could do that. I know I could."

Jess stood up and sauntered over to look over Tacy's shoulder at App's drawing. Now that Tacy studied it, she could see it was some kind of cannon.

"Sir, I was thinking if y'all were really

wanting to have a competition, a catapult competition would be fun," Jess said. "I'd kinda like to try my hand at one of those… and since this will be Mule Hollow's first time for a competition, one category of chunkin would be an easier way for anybody to get involved."

"I don't know," Applegate mused, spitting a sunflower husk into a spittoon. "I was thinkin' more along the lines of a cannon. I kinda like the idea of that."

Jess chuckled, but when Tacy glanced at him his eyes were serious. "On many of those cannons, the teams have engineers and such to make sure no one gets hurt. Compressed air that powerful can be dangerous."

"You sayin' I wouldn't be careful?" App barked, throwing his thin shoulders back.

"Well, no, sir. I just meant, well, you know, other people. Not you, sir. You would do just fine, I'm sure."

"Yer darn tootin' I would be. Did I ever tell you I worked the oil rigs fer thirty years and had the top safety record?"

"Well, no, sir, I didn't know that."

Tacy hid a smile, enjoying poor Jess's flustered state.

"He's right," Stanley said, finally jumping in to help him out. "We wouldn't want nobody gettin' hurt over a little bit of fun."

"I'm for the catapults," Norma Sue said. "After all, we don't have a whole lot of time before we get this little contest up and running. What do y'all think?"

App and Stanley looked at each other and nodded. "Agreed," they said in unison.

It was decided that all competition would be with catapults and they'd only do a local competition for the first year. Anyone around Mule Hollow could compete, but they wouldn't be advertising for anyone else to sign up. Maybe next year, Applegate said, and Tacy could see he had visions of cannons in his mischievous old eyes.

"You seem worried," Tacy said in a hushed voice a few minutes later when she brought Jess his lunch. He leaned close.

"I didn't want them to get hurt. Did you see that thing App was drawing? It was a monster."

She smiled at his ingenuity. "You know, Jess, I'm impressed. That was a smooth move on your part."

He gave her a wink. "Impressed enough to agree to that date?"

She laughed. "I've told you, cowboy. I'm not dating. Even if you have managed to impress me," she drawled and returned his teasing wink just as Brent walked into the diner. She met his stare across the room and her temper, which had dissipated, shot right back up like a fever spike. "Where are all your buddies today?" she asked Jess, watching as Brent strode toward the counter. He could sit there and wait a few minutes.

"They got stuck on fence patrol so they're tailgating on the job. I thought I'd have you all to myself today. Boy, was I wrong."

"How did you manage to get out of that?" she asked, glancing back at Brent.

"I couldn't miss my ballet lessons. Today was the fitting for my tutu, so Clint let me come to town."

"Oh, well, that's good," she said, pulling her gaze back and finding Jess looking amused. *"What?"*

"I just told you I came to town for ballet lessons and a tutu."

Tacy frowned. "Well, why in the world would you tell me something crazy like that?"

"I guess to find out why you can't take your eyes off that new bronc buster."

Tacy scowled at Jess. "I just glanced at the guy."

"Yeah, and my name is Elvis Presley," he said grumpily. "Do I have some competition? You know I've won my fair share of rodeos, if that's what's impressing you."

"Hardly. I already told you, you're wasting your time with me. I'm not dating you and certainly not Mr. Congeniality over there." She gave Jess a firm nod. Then, taking a deep breath, she walked toward Brent. She might as well get this over with.

Chapter Six

Brent wasn't sure why he'd decided to come into town for lunch. He'd known Tacy would be working the rush hour and that she would still be highly ticked off at him.

But he'd come anyway.

She'd been having a good time smiling and winking at her boyfriend when he walked in. One glance in his direction and she'd chilled up like an ice cube.

"So what'll it be?" she asked, coming to a stop in front of him just as Sam came out of the kitchen.

"Afternoon, Brent. You come back for some more meat loaf? Or to see my purdy waitress?"

Brent held up his hands in surrender. "No meat loaf. I came for a burger," he declared, then shifted his focus to Tacy. "I also came to see your pretty waitress."

She looked like he'd caught her off guard when her stony gaze faltered.

With a wry smile, Sam said, "Well, don't mind me. I got yer burger to cook." Chuckling all the way, he disappeared into the kitchen.

Brent watched Tacy grab a glass and busy herself filling it with iced tea. She must have automatically assumed he wanted tea since he'd ordered it last time. That didn't stop the unexpected zing of pleasure that shot through him when he realized she'd remembered his drink of choice—but he ignored it. "I came to apologize for making you mad."

She hesitated before setting the glass down in front of him, letting it hover above the napkin momentarily as his words sank in. Then she plunked it down and crossed her arms. "Something tells me that apology doesn't include remorse enough to offer an invitation to help me learn how to train those colts."

She was tenacious. "No. I won't do that. I have my reasons."

"And?" she said, lifting a quizzical brow.

"And I don't really care to explain myself."

She opened her mouth to say something,

then clamped it shut. Her green eyes flashed. "Typical male apology. My way or no way," she huffed, then swung away and stomped around the counter, grabbing a pitcher of iced tea on her way to make the rounds.

Grinding his teeth, he watched as she cheerily refilled glasses. This was not going the way he'd hoped. There was no reason for this feud to continue. If the woman would only see reason!

Across the room, Applegate and Stanley were getting ready to leave when App caught his eye and strode over. "You ain't doin' so good," the eagle-eyed older man said loudly, turning several heads their way—including those of Norma Sue and her crew.

Suddenly feeling as if he were onstage, Brent turned his back to the room and picked up his tea. "Don't know what you're talking about," he said, giving App a sideways glance, hoping he'd drop it. The twinkle in App's eyes told him he wasn't going to be that lucky. Or that he didn't care that their conversation could be heard by almost everyone in the diner.

"Jest ask her out. You know ya want to."

Brent decided that not answering was the

smartest move. He was relieved when Tacy came swinging around the bar—but she just dropped off the tea, shot App a glare and marched straight into the kitchen, leaving him staring after her.

"Never mind." App chuckled. "She don't look like she'd go out with ya anyway. You know anything about catapults?"

Not at all sure what catapults and dates with Tacy had to do with each other, Brent was leery of answering. "Not really," he said. Tacy came out of the kitchen, hamburger in one hand and Sam following. They both stopped in front of him as Tacy slapped his meal on the counter.

"Me and Stanley are gonna build a punkin chunker and need some fellas ta join our team. You look like you could use some friends—seein' as how yor new in town and done started miffing certain folks."

"That's an understatement," Tacy grumbled and walked back into the dining area, distributing lunch bills to the tables.

Stanley had joined Applegate and now Brent was looking at three wrinkled, grinning old codgers. "I'll help out if y'all promise to lay off."

"Good deal," Stanley said. "Meet us out at App's place after church on Sunday. We gotta git to play practice out at the Barn Theater right now. We have a show out there tanight and two shows tomorrow so we ain't got no time open 'til Sunday."

That said, they headed toward the door, stopping at Norma Sue's table to tell her, loud enough for folks all over the county to hear, that they were getting up a winning team and she and Esther Mae were going down.

"What in the world was all that?" Brent asked, turning back to Sam.

"Some friendly competition. I think Tacy is on Norma Sue, Esther Mae and my Adela's team. You better watch out or you might just set off a real feud."

Brent listened as Sam explained the "punkin chunkin" contest. It sounded like good fun. "So there'll be more teams than just Norma Sue's and Applegate's?"

"That's the plan. But them two teams are what'll count. It's gonna be war. Jess thar— that cowboy who's talkin' to yor Tacy with that twinkle in his eye—he suggested ever'body build the same category of contraption. The catapult."

Brent had taken a bite of his burger and glanced over his shoulder to see Tacy chatting it up with the cowboy she'd been winking at when he walked into the diner. She was saying something, and he could tell by the tilt of her head and the light in her eyes that it was sassy. He took a couple more bites then stood up, rammed his hand into his pocket and pulled out his money clip, peeling off bills to pay for his meal.

"You leavin' so soon?" Sam asked.

"It was good, Sam, but I need to get back to work."

"You didn't even eat half of it."

"Not hungry, I guess. Have a good day," he said, snagging up his hat from the stool beside him. He didn't miss the grin on Sam's face. But it wasn't the speculation that bothered him as he strode out of the diner and climbed into his truck. It was seeing Tacy flirting with that cowboy that had his gut twisting up in knots. He told himself all the way back to the pens that he was a fool. Yet there was just something about Tacy that reached inside him and made him want to get to know her better.

But that wasn't happening. They had a barrier between them that couldn't be breached... he wouldn't let it.

Tacy didn't work at Sam's on Saturdays. Sam's other part-time waitress and cook worked Saturdays and some weeknights. Tacy normally spent all day at the corral working with Rabbit. She didn't plan to change that just because Brent was there.

The other days she'd gone there after her shift, dreading running into him, and was relieved when he'd stayed in the corral while she stayed in the barn and the pasture, well out of his way. It had worked out just fine. For now.

It wasn't going to last, though. She was too curious about what was going on inside that corral. Too curious about Brent. The cowboy had reasons for not wanting her in that pen, and she'd decided it was time to find out just exactly what they were. If she understood, then she could better figure out how to get around it.

Seven in the morning, and he was already in the pen with the chestnut. Tacy sat in her truck and watched him lift the saddle and place it on the colt's back. Three days ago that horse had jumped and flinched. Today it seemed calm and comfortable. From the distance, she could see how Brent worked with that same easy, relaxed movement he used with the other horse. Birdy, the traitor, had taken up permanent residence by Brent and lay flopped on the ground with her chin on her paws, watching him with adoring eyes. The man just had a way of drawing a woman's attention. She sighed and watched as he placed a booted foot in the stirrup. The horse immediately stepped sideways. Brent went with it, keeping his hand on the saddle horn, his boot in the stirrup and hopping along on the other boot. Though she was too far away to hear him, she could tell he was speaking to the horse. Then, with unbelievable grace, he was in the saddle. Easy, breezy, no big deal—or so it seemed. That wasn't the most impressive part, either. Oh, no, it was that he was sitting in the saddle of a fairly *calm* horse. He walked it around the pen. No bucking, no dancing, no running.

Tacy smiled all the way to her toes. Wow. Brent was good, and she was going to learn how to do that. Oh, *yeah.*

Striding across the yard, she bent to pet

Birdy. "Is it getting close, girl?" she asked, though she knew it was. Any day now puppies would arrive. Tacy could hardly wait. Brent was acting like he hadn't seen her walk up, but she knew he knew she was there.

"Stubborn man," she mumbled, folding her arms and resting her elbows on the corral, daring him not to acknowledge her. Finally, he turned his head her way. Feeling exceptionally prickly, she lifted her hand slightly and waved daintily. To her surprise, he raised his chin in acknowledgment.

Stepping away from the fence, she decided she needed to tend to Rabbit. She wanted Brent to teach her how to break horses, and absolutely nothing more. The man was too hard, too stubborn. She'd dealt with his kind all her life. Her dad was the same way and had raised her four brothers with the same outlook. So why, she wanted to know, was she thinking that she'd like to get to know him better? It was crazy. She entered the barn and headed to Rabbit's stall.

"You didn't stay long."

His low rumble shocked her, and she spun around to find him standing in the doorway of the barn looking better than anybody had a right to look. He wore ragged jeans, a T-shirt that stretched across his strong shoulders like a second skin and that beat-up hat that had seen better days. It all combined beautifully with his strong jaw, lips that were hitched slightly to one side and eyes that said he was just as wary—and interested—as she was. Tacy ran her hand along Rabbit's saddle.

"I decided that irritating you wasn't on my agenda today. You were too impressive out there."

He relaxed a shoulder against the entrance and crossed his arms, watching her. "That's something new. You sure you can make it through the day doing that?"

He didn't acknowledge her compliment, but she laughed at his unexpected humor. "I made it just fine before you showed up around here. I'm pretty sure I can manage."

He smiled. "I'm sure you can."

She gave an exaggerated gasp. "Was that a compliment?"

"I don't know? Was it?"

"You know you like me."

"Do you flirt with everyone?"

"Oh, so now you're getting personal," she

teased, enjoying herself more than she probably should. "Am I flirting?"

His eyes sparkled with amusement. "You're not?"

"I don't know, am I?"

He raised a brow. "Do you flirt with everyone?"

That gave her pause.… "You mean Jess?"

"Is that his name?"

This was interesting. She thought he'd seen her winking at Jess earlier at the diner, but she hadn't expected him to ask her about it. "Why are you asking about my social life? Do *not* tell me you're thinking about asking me out." His eyes shifted slightly and she knew he'd been thinking exactly that. "Oh, no." She half laughed. "I'll tell you the same as I've told Jess and all the other cowboys looking to date me—I don't date."

"I wasn't going to ask you out," he denied.

She laughed, not believing him for one moment. "Then why the nosy question? And why do you look so startled by my straight-up answer?" *Cowboys*—they were so easy to read, especially after being raised with four brothers. She had his number, and she knew it.

He did, too. Caught in his bluff, he snatched

his hat from his head and rammed his free hand through his thick, straight, sandy-brown hair.

She planted herself in front of him. "You're *flustered,*" she pressed, looking up at him intently, unable to resist teasing him.

His gaze darkened and dropped to her lips, then jerked back to meet her eyes.

Suddenly Tacy realized that she might not be as much in control of the situation as she'd believed!

Brent wanted to tug Tacy into his arms and kiss her sassy mouth. This thing they had between them was like an electric current. Dangerous and powerful. He leaned toward her, every fiber in him intent on finding out if a kiss would be electric, when she slapped a palm to his chest, flattening it firmly in place.

"Whoa, cowboy," she warned. "I said I don't date. And I certainly don't kiss cowboys who've told me they have no respect for me."

"What? Where did you get that?"

She cocked a brow, flipped her ponytail over her shoulder and strode back to Rabbit's stall.

He followed at a slower pace, stunned by her accusation. "I never said I didn't respect you."

She opened the gate and entered the stall, glancing over her shoulder to pin him with her stare. "Sure you did. You won't let me in that arena with those horses." She opened the back gate and shooed Rabbit out into the back run before turning to face him. "You won't let me near them or teach me how to break them. That's like shouting at me that you have no respect for me."

"That's not true."

"Oh, yeah? Then explain to me what it does mean."

She stepped by him, grabbed hold of the wheelbarrow and rake used to clean the stall and pushed past him into the stall to begin working.

"Say something," she said. "You must have a reason for being so against a woman learning how to break horses. Since I'm the woman it's affecting at the moment, don't you think you owe me an explanation?"

She had a point, though he didn't like it very much. "What exactly do you know about me?" he asked, following her as she pushed the wheelbarrow outside to dump it. He took the handles and was surprised when she stepped back and let him empty the contents. "If you're trying to flit through all the sordid details you know and pick the things you think won't make me mad, don't bother," he said finally. "Some of it was true, but most of it wasn't. What I'm asking is what you know about when I dropped out of the NRF competition."

There was a feed trough built along the back side of the barn, and Tacy sat on the edge of it now, looking up at him with intent eyes. He waited.

"Look," she huffed. "I only know what was on the cover of those magazines. That you had an on-again, off-again thing with a TV star named Jessica and that you were photographed with a new girl every other week in between that relationship. What I know about you leaving the NRF is less. I know you had a family emergency. The *only* article I ever read was one in the *Horseman* and you know that is a respectable magazine. You gave the interview, after all, so you know it didn't deal with your dating life or your family. It was about you and your run for the National Rodeo Finals. Plus, you happened to mention that you loved meat loaf." She raised her hand as if giving a solemn oath. "That's the honest truth." She sighed, letting her hand down. "I admit, I did believe what I saw on the front covers of those magazines. I'm sorry. Really."

His anger subsided. He couldn't help but like her frankness. With each barrier they erased between them, the harder it was not to want to get to know her better…and she'd just said she didn't date. Why was that?

"Forget it," he said. "I'm the one who set myself up for the public scrutiny. I was a regular jerk back then…you don't have anything to be sorry about."

She studied him, silence stretching between them like a soft breeze, promising cooler weather. Brent wrestled with his growing attraction to her. Looking at her, he couldn't think straight. He wondered if she had this effect on everyone.

"So," she said after a minute. "What about all of that made you not want women near horses?"

Chapter Seven

"Do you want to go for a ride?"

Brent's question startled Tacy. She had expected evasiveness, but a ride… Pushing away from the feed trough she'd been half sitting on, she gave him a playful smile. "Are you kidding? I'm always up for a ride." She whistled and Rabbit came trotting up from the pasture. "You *are* planning to answer my question—not to take me out in the pastures and do away with me so I'll stop bothering you?"

He laughed, short and quick. "No devious plans on my part, I promise. And yes, I'll explain. You've been straight with me, so you deserve the same. First, let's ride."

"I like the sound of that." Tacy sauntered

into the barn with Rabbit trailing. Birdy, who'd been abnormally quiet today, waddled behind Brent as he headed toward the pen where his big bay stood.

A few minutes later, Tacy rode Rabbit down the barn alley and out into the morning sunshine. Brent was petting Birdy and straightened as Tacy rode up.

"She's getting ready to have her pups," he said as he swung into the saddle.

"You read my mind," she agreed, moving Rabbit into a slow trot toward the open pasture back behind the cabin. Soon they were riding easily beside each other in companionable silence. Tacy stole a few glances at the mystifying cowboy. He seemed totally preoccupied as they let the horses warm up.

"This is where I let Rabbit pretend he's in the Kentucky Derby," she said after a few minutes, drawing Brent's attention. She grinned and gave Rabbit his lead—which was all the horse had been waiting for. Leaning into the wind, she flew with the horse down the soft trail, heading toward the distant trees. Tacy loved the feel of the animal as it moved powerfully and gracefully over the land. As the wind filled

Tacy's lungs and rushed through her hair, she couldn't help smiling. This was her element. This was where, when she'd been a kid and her daddy had refused to let her work alongside him and her brothers, she would come and let all her frustrations loose in the wind. On Rabbit's back she felt as if she could conquer the world. She also felt at peace…as if God were whispering in her ear that she was headed in the right direction.

Now, sailing across Pace's pasture with Brent in hot pursuit, things felt as if they were coming together. Brent drew near as Rabbit slowed and she laughed at his expression. "Don't look all indignant and *don't* tell me this is dangerous! I've been riding like this since I was knee-high."

He grinned. "I was going to tell you that you sit your horse well."

She gaped at him. "Wow, blow me over. That was a real compliment."

"It happens. Where did you learn to ride like that?"

"My dad. And my older brothers. They all live on the ranch down in central Texas."

"So if you're from a ranch and you have that

many brothers, why'd you have to come here to find someone to teach you to break horses?"

She scowled. "Because my dad and my fool brothers think the way you do. Which is just plain crazy. They think it's okay for me to ride. Okay for me to train already broke, tamed horses. I came here because I'm good and I know it. I have a good seat on a horse, and I have a natural feel for them and I want to work a horse from beginning to end." She shot him a determined look. "And I *will* learn. I know why they don't want to teach me. I'm just not sure why you don't think I could learn."

Brent halted his horse, and she did the same.

He took a deep breath, giving Tacy the feeling he was forcing himself to speak. "I have a little sister. She was nineteen when I was home between rodeos two years ago."

His jaw seized up. He shifted in the saddle and stared from Tacy to the distant trees. The blue sky and the soft breeze belied the sudden tenseness of the moment. Tacy felt it, and her stomach tightened.

After a second, he continued. "I'd brought a horse home with me. Tina was home from college and, as she often did when we were home at the same time, she came down to the barn to watch me. I'd been drinking...."

Brent's expression clouded over and she knew then that this cut deep. She wanted to reach across and comfort him. "She sounds like me," she said softly, trying to think of something that would ease the moment. Anything that would help take away the torment that was glowing behind his pale eyes. She wished she hadn't pushed for this.

"You do remind me of her in some ways," he said. "She wanted to try her luck on my horse. Thought she could do it. Thought it would be great fun." He swallowed hard and rubbed the back of his neck.

"I let her. I helped her into the stirrups. The horse bolted, tossed her on her head and broke her neck."

"Did—did she die?" Tacy gasped.

He gave a terse shake of his head. "No, she lived. By the grace of God she lived...but she was in the hospital for months. We didn't think she'd ever walk again."

He started walking his horse and Tacy urged Rabbit forward. There was no doubt in her mind that he blamed himself completely for his sister's tragic accident. "That's why you dropped out of the rodeo finals."

"Because I was a cocky, drunk jerk, I nearly killed my sister—that set my priorities straight instantly."

It wasn't any of her business. Still, Tacy couldn't help feeling horrible. For his sister. For him. For his parents. She could only imagine how such a tragic accident could affect a family—either make it stronger or tear it apart. "So you stayed home and helped out."

He nodded. "Yeah, I did. But things haven't been good. Tina's neck finally started healing, but it was touch and go there for a while. The doctors say she'll make a full recovery—I don't believe it. And my dad doesn't, either, and can't forgive me for that—not that I'm asking him to. I completely understand where he's coming from."

Tacy could only imagine if one of her brothers had let her on a rough stock horse. Even if she hadn't been injured, her dad would have been furious. "It sounds like our fathers are very much alike."

"Really?"

"Yeah, I was just thinking that if one of my brothers had let me so much as put my boot in the stirrup of a rough colt, my dad would have had his hide pinned to the barn door."

"Your dad's a good man, then."

Tacy liked that he respected their fathers' attitudes. She didn't agree with her dad's outlook on her abilities, but she respected him all the same. He was doing what he thought was best for her.

A snake slithered across the rutted road they were following and both their horses side-stepped. It was no big deal, but catching Brent watching her reaction and how she stayed in control—that *was* a big deal. The man was practically grading her abilities as they rode. She understood why now, but Tacy knew her own capabilities. She was good. Real good. He wouldn't find anything to hold against her, if that was what he was looking for. "Yes, my dad is the best. I respect him more than anyone, but I refuse to let his need to protect and coddle me stop me from following my dreams. I'm *good,* Brent. I'm assuming your sister's accident and your feelings of responsibility are the reasons you refuse to teach me?"

"It's not negotiable."

Tacy bit her lip and said a prayer for Brent. She felt like there was even more he hadn't said, and she worried that it was no use pushing the issue. Yet she felt a gentle nudge to say something to ease his distress. But what?

Being at a loss for words was just plain weird for Tacy. If it was God who was nudging her, wouldn't He also be giving her the words to say? Instead, her mind was blank as she met Brent's grim expression.

"Tell me more about your sister's recovery."

"It's been hard on her. Months in the hospital, then months of physical therapy…"

"Why do you hesitate?"

"I pushed her pretty hard. Mom and Dad worried that I was too hard on her. But I felt that if she didn't give it her all, she might not recover fully."

So that was it. "You and your parents clashed over that?"

He nodded. "When Tina started complaining and getting upset, I decided maybe I was letting my guilt push me into being too hard on her. That's when I left."

"Where did you go?"

"To Idaho. A cowboy can get lost in the Great Basin…that's what I always heard, anyway. I knew a guy looking for wranglers through the winter. That's where I met Pace."

"Y'all worked together?"

"Yes, Pace was practically a legend. We worked adjacent sections so sometimes we'd work together. Out there in the winter you're pretty much on your own. Both of us had little one-room cabins—more like shacks with no electricity."

"No electricity? None?"

He gave a small smile, and for the first time since they'd started riding the tension eased. "It wasn't so bad, really. I had plenty of firewood."

Tacy laughed. "You're a cowboy. I'm sure it was just like going back to your roots."

"I liked it. Not gonna say I'd want to live that way forever. But it was where I needed to be at the time. Tacy, do you believe that God puts you where you need to be when you need to be there?"

"Very much so." She looked at him and wondered what it was God was trying to show her now, in this moment. She'd come to Mule Hollow with plans and they'd been totally turned upside down. When Brent had shown up and refused to help her she'd been so miffed. Now, after talking to him, she felt assured there had been no mistake. There was a reason she was here with Brent, though she didn't have a clue what that reason was yet.

Surely it wasn't to irritate the cowboy, because that was pretty much what she'd been doing. And though they were talking now, she had no misconception that once she pushed him some more to let her help with those horses, they'd be right back to square one. And she would push. She still had to follow her dream.

Though she felt bad for him and even empathized with him, Tacy would not back down. She was not his sister. She'd make him see that somehow.

Brent had surprised himself when he'd started telling Tacy about his family issues. He'd meant to reveal as little as possible— just enough so that she would see how futile her efforts were to try to change his stance on teaching a woman how to break a bronc. She'd truly seemed to care as he told his story. The only person he'd ever revealed so much to had been Pace.

Something about Tacy drew him out, despite their difference of opinion. But she wasn't the type to give in—and even after telling her his story, he had no illusions that she'd say okay and give up. And he would not give in.

"Do you and your dad speak?" she asked.

He considered the question as he turned the horse off the road and onto a trail leading through the trees. "No," he said at last. "I haven't spoken to Dad in about six months. He likes it that way."

"Surely not."

The disbelief was strong in her voice.

"It's for the best. I let my dad down in more ways than one." He wasn't about to air the rest of his dirty laundry for Tacy to give more gasps of disbelief. Her sympathy was the last thing he was looking for. Her cooperation—now that he would take gladly.

"You said your dad sounds a lot like my dad. Do you speak to your dad?"

"Yes, of course I do. He's not happy about me going against his wishes to pursue my dream of breaking and training horses. But he's proud that I have his spirit and drive and won't take no for an answer. You see, I think that if I learn it somewhere else, it's different in his mind than if he or my brothers teach me. It takes the responsibility off him—not that he'd ever admit that. He still rants and raves about it and is more than pleased about how this has turned out for me down here so far. He keeps telling me to stop wasting time and come home to the ranch. My dad and my brothers have a custom stirrup company, and there's a great job waiting for me in the family business."

There was no mistaking the way she felt about that. Brent glanced at her to confirm that Tacy Jones had no intention of ever going into the stirrup business. That was plain enough.

"Your family is *Jones Custom Stirrups?*"

"One and the same," she quipped.

"Those are great stirrups."

"Yup. They've been good for the family."

"But not you?"

"Not what I want to do with my life. I'm proud of Dad and the business. It's just not my dream."

"So when did you know that training horses was what you wanted to do?"

"I got serious about it when I was a senior in high school. That's when I realized I had a mind of my own and a will that I could start asserting. Believe me, when you're raised by a protective dad and four older brothers, that isn't something that just jumps out at you."

"I can't picture you as a gal who didn't assert herself. Quiet and obedient don't compute when thinking of you." Brent chuckled.

Her laughter joined his and reverberated through the woods. "Believe me, I was never quiet. Obedient could be argued—my teachers would attest to that. But I did know my limitations when Dad put his foot down. I knew not to cross him."

"But as an adult it's different?"

She nodded, but said nothing.

"So you know how to work a horse and train it?"

"Dad didn't have a problem with that. It was the breaking that he objected to. Sound familiar?"

He shot her a droll look, hiking a brow. He'd been observing her for days, and everything she said about natural talent and a natural seat for the horse was true. If she was a man, he'd be glad to take her talent to the next level. Pace had helped him do that while they were in Idaho by sharing his expertise as far as gentle breaking was concerned. Brent couldn't help wondering if he'd known more—if he'd had the horse a little more ready to receive a rider—would Tina have been spared all the pain and trouble she'd been through over the last two years? It was something he'd never know. Of course, the one thing he *did* know was that if he'd listened to his dad and hadn't been so full of himself and alcohol, nothing would have happened that night. He wouldn't have let Tina get on that horse. He would have known it was a bad idea. "Your dad sounds like he loves you very much."

"Never a doubt there. But that can't stop me from living my dream, my choice."

Brent wouldn't have expected any other answer from her. "So you loaded up, came down here where Pace has agreed to help you and, as luck would have it, you ended up with me. The guy who feels just like your dad. Only I have the tragic consequences to back up my convictions."

Tacy reined in her horse, and he did, too. She stared at him with thoughtful eyes. "Actually, I don't believe in luck. Or coincidence. I could leave here today, head down to any number of ranches I know of and learn to break horses. Or I could sign up for weekend workshops taught by talented cowboys. This is not my only option. I *chose* to come here. I wanted to learn from Pace because he is a legend. The best."

Everything she said rang true. She could go learn to break horses anywhere. And, okay, he'd admit she seemed like she'd be good enough. She was a better rider than Tina had been. Still, if he put Tacy on that horse and something happened, it would be his responsibility. And he couldn't take that.

"But," Tacy continued, studying him hard, "Pace had to leave, and now you're here. And you know what?" She smiled, tilting her heart-shaped face slightly as solemn green eyes locked with his.

"What?" he asked.

"I believe we're here for a reason. I don't think this is a chance meeting. I can feel it. I think maybe God has brought us together for a purpose—a purpose *other* than for you to aggravate me."

Chapter Eight

Tacy wasn't sure what she'd been thinking the day before when she'd blurted out that God had brought them together for a reason—a purpose. Brent had just looked at her like she was crazy and she'd actually felt a bit insane even thinking such a thing! She'd refused to elaborate, telling him she wasn't sure why she felt that way. She just had a hunch…and her hunches were usually right. Thankfully, he'd laughed at that and then let it go, probably assuming she'd only been teasing—little did he know that she hadn't been.

It was easy to see he was hurting—that he was eaten up with remorse and guilt over his sister. And this thing with his dad—well, that was going to eat him alive. Really, she and her dad might not see eye to eye but she could not imagine anything so horrible happening that they no longer spoke to each other. Tacy felt a strong sense of loss for Brent and her heart ached for him.

When they'd arrived back at the barn, she'd wanted to watch him work, but she held back. She could tell he wasn't sure what to think about her not hassling him. Though she still wasn't afraid of anything happening to her, she did respect that Brent had a reason for not wanting her in that arena.

So she'd left him alone.

Thoughts of him distracted her the rest of the day and she ended up sitting out on the back porch, staring at the moon and contemplating everything banging around inside her head.

Her daddy always said she could be sassy as a new colt kicking up his feet on a fresh spring day when she wanted something, or quiet as a mouse when something was on her mind. Brent was definitely on her mind—the pain in his eyes, the attraction she felt for him—the matching attraction she saw reflected in his eyes when he looked at her. Needless to say, she didn't sleep well and was dragging her feet as she stopped to talk to Esther Mae this morning in front of the Sunday-school annex.

"Esther Mae, how's y'all's contraption comin' along?" Applegate asked as he strode up to the two of them.

"Goodness, App," Tacy said, giving him a quick hug. "You are lookin' dapper in your Sunday best." That won her a grin and a lifted right brow.

"Thank ya, little lady. Yor lookin' like a fresh spring day yourself."

Tacy glanced down at her moss-green dress. "Thanks."

"Now, App," Esther Mae broke in, "you know I'm not going to give away any of our secrets, so don't even think about sweet-talking me. And don't bother asking Hank if he knows them, either. I've threatened his life if he so much as opens his mouth about anything he hears or sees at the house."

Applegate grunted. "I ain't about ta sweet-talk you. And Hank done told me you'd put him in the doghouse if he said anything."

Esther Mae smiled. "My Hank is a smart man."

Applegate scowled at her as he turned his

sharp gaze toward Tacy. "Have you seen the design?"

Tacy had to smile as his face turned into a cascade of wrinkles. "No, sir, not yet, but I'm going out there later." She leaned in conspiratorially. "If you'll give me a big ole smile I might be willing to give you a few insights. How's *your* contraption comin' along?"

"Hey!" Esther Mae squealed. "You'd better do no such a thing."

"Hang loose, Esther Mae. I'm just teasing. You people are taking this far too seriously."

"You bet your daddy's boots we are," Stanley said, coming out of the annex and catching the tail end of the conversation. "Who don't take men versus women serious? Us fellas gotta win or we look bad. Ain't that right, App?"

"Shore 'nuff."

Esther Mae harrumphed. "I hate to break it to you boys, but there's no amount of winnin' that's gonna make y'all look good."

Tacy covered her mouth with her hand and held in a laugh. The "boys" glared at Esther Mae. She lifted a hand and patted her hair. "Now me—well, Lacy has done a lovely job of making me look fantabulous."

Applegate's bushy brows became one. "Fantabu-what?" he practically shouted.

"Fantabulous. Do you like my new color?"

Stanley and App looked at Esther Mae as if she'd just spoken in a foreign language.

"It's bull's-eye red, Esther Mae," App said at last.

"Men!" Esther Mae rolled her eyes. "In case you hadn't noticed, boys, all reds are not created equal. This is Chili Pepper red, for your information."

Tacy gave her a thumbs-up. "Perfect for you."

"I thought so. It's a tad spicier than my natural color, but I figure these days the brighter the better."

"I'm with you on that," Tacy said. "Maybe we should paint our catapult red or something equally bright."

"We gonna paint ours?" Stanley asked App, who just headed toward the annex shaking his head.

"I guess that's a no." Stanley grinned, then followed his friend.

"They're a tad touchy when it comes to this competition," Tacy said.

Esther Mae waved a hand. "The thought of

getting beat by women terrifies ole App." She grinned. "Of course, he's not too fond of losing to a man, either, yet that happens with checkers every day."

"Now, Esther Mae. You know it's the thought of being beaten by you and Norma Sue that's not sitting well with him."

"This is true," she said, looking amused. "It's fun tormenting him."

Tacy laughed. "Seems we have something in common as far as men are concerned."

"My Hank gets on me all the time when I tease him, but he says that since App and Stanley give me such a hard time, they deserve all the torture I can dish out to them."

Hank came out of the annex. He was a short man with a paunch and a pleasant grin. "There you are," he said to Esther Mae, then gave Tacy an affable smile. "Mornin' to you, Tacy. Class is about to start, so I thought I'd better come see where Esther Mae got to."

"I didn't get lost, just ambushed by Applegate."

Hank looked past them toward App and Stanley, who had stopped to talk to a group of men. "He asked you about that contraption, didn't he?"

"You know he did. It's driving him crazy."

Hank shook his head. "She loves giving that man a hard time. If I didn't know she was so crazy about me, I might have call to get jealous."

Tacy paused before heading toward the singles' class. "I don't think you have anything to worry about, Hank."

Esther Mae took her husband's arm and squeezed it fondly. "I only have eyes for you, Hank. Even after all these years. It's amazing, isn't it?"

"Yep. I'm a lucky man."

App and Stanley came into the building. "You jest keep a tellin' yerself that," App said, adjusting his hearing aid as he passed them.

Hank and Esther Mae chuckled as they followed App and Stanley down the hall to their Sunday-school class.

Tacy watched them go, hanging back, feeling unusually chicken-hearted today. Earlier, when she'd first arrived, she'd seen Brent heading her way and she'd changed direction. Why? Avoiding someone was certainly not her style. But after yesterday—she couldn't believe she'd actually opened her big mouth and told him she was in his life for a reason. Crazy talk—that's what it was. Wasn't it? She breathed a quick prayer, asking God to calm her nerves, then entered the classroom. Immediately, she saw Brent and her crazy heart started doing the rumba inside her chest. "Okay, God, I'm trusting you to help me get through this," Tacy mumbled inwardly.

She took a deep breath and gave Brent and the fellas he was talking to as easy a grin as she could muster. Then she chose the seat right in front of Brent. She refused to let herself avoid him any longer. Fear of anything was just something she wouldn't accept. Even this unexpected attraction to Brent. She could handle it.

The last thing she'd expected was for Jess to walk in and take the empty seat beside her.

Brent let go of the table saw's trigger and set the saw to the side. "Fellas, I am not going to try to spy on Tacy so I can learn how the ladies are building their catapult." Brent had come out to App's straight after church and so far it had been a miserable day. He'd been forced to sit and watch Jess-the-flirt giving Tacy his best shot all through Sunday school.

Didn't the man know you weren't supposed to flirt in church? It was ridiculous.

The cowboy didn't even come to church. He was too busy hanging out on Saturday nights over in Ranger at the bars. Brent hadn't been able to keep from asking around about the cowboy after seeing Tacy wink at him in the diner. It was obvious that Jess had come today for one reason and one reason only—and it wasn't to encounter God. No, it was to encounter someone with copper hair that fell midway down the back of her chair and bounced with life every time she nodded or chuckled at something Jess said to her.

So she liked wild cowboys. Kinda hypocritical on her part, seeing as how she'd been down on him about the tabloid covers. Thing was, he'd learned and left that life behind… and here she was smiling and teasing Jess.

"What has you in such an all-fired bad mood, anyway?" Applegate asked.

Brent scowled. "I'm not."

Stanley spat a sunflower seed onto the barn floor. "Then I'd hate ta see ya in a bad mood if this ain't it."

"Yup." Applegate snorted. "I know what's

eatin' ya. You seen that Jess at church, didn't ya?"

Stanley crossed his arms. "That boy ain't walked through them doors ever before. Probably too hungover most Sunday mornings ta ever consider it."

It was none of his business, Brent told himself. But it bothered him. He was attracted to Tacy—there was no denying it. But he had no hold on her and no reason to be aggravated that she seemed to be her usual sassy self this morning while he'd felt all ill-tempered and…jealous. There. It was out. He'd been jealous.

He grabbed his measuring tape and strung it along the two-by-four. "What's that measurement?"

Applegate plucked up the drawing and squinted at his handwriting. "Seventy-two inches," he said.

Brent marked it with his pencil, snapped the tape so it would recoil then dropped it to the table and picked up the saw. "You fellas really believe God orchestrates our lives?"

App's bushy brows crinkled as he rubbed his chin. "Thar's different opinions on that. I believe He's in control…but I don't believe

He sits back and works me like a puppet. I got free will. I mess up all the time. If ya haven't noticed, I kin get purdy cantankerous, too."

"Ever'body's noticed," Stanley drawled. "The way I see it, God's got us here and we're learning as we go. If He was guiding our every move, thar would be nothin' fer us to learn. Now don't get me wrong. I thank the Bible is purdy clear that He knows what our choices are goin' ta be. That don't mean He orchestrates our lives, though."

Brent tapped his finger on the edge of the saw trigger, but didn't engage it. "What about sending people into your life when you need them?"

"Oh, He definitely does that," App said. "No doubt about it."

"Yeah, seen plenty of that in our own lives," Stanley agreed. "Not to mention here in Mule Hollow. Now that I thank about it, that sort of contradicts what I jest said. Still, jest 'cause He puts us in people's paths don't mean He uses us like puppets. Why?"

"Tacy said yesterday she thought she was put in my life for a reason." Just as he'd expected, both older men started grinning.

App was the first to speak. "She done

told all them cowboys in the diner that she ain't here ta date. How'd you get her ta change her mind?"

"I'm not dating her. She'd probably kick me in the knee if I asked her."

Stanley's grin turned to a grimace. "You ain't asked her out? Are ya addled in the brain? Been tossed on yer noggin a time or two too many?"

"*No*. This has nothing to do with me being attracted to her."

"Hear that, App? He admits he's attracted to her."

"The boy's got hope, then."

Brent pulled the trigger and welcomed the blaring grind of the saw. Why had he opened his big mouth? He finished cutting the board and took the plunge. "So what's up with her not dating?"

"She ain't interested, so she says," Stanley said.

"But why is that?" She'd pretty much told him to back off the other day in the barn. Sure, she'd said she didn't date and that she'd made it clear to all the cowboys, but the woman was flirting and winking in the diner all the time. Especially with Jess. Did she not realize that kind of behavior was sending mixed messages? He was certainly confused.

Applegate studied him. "She says she's got things ta get done before she puts marryin' some old cowboy and raisin' a family at the top of her list."

So her career was top priority. Horse training. Things became clearer to him. She was serious about this horse business.

"Why don't you push to get ta know her better?" Applegate suggested, taking the finished board from the table. "Young gal like her don't need ta be sittin' home alone."

"She's sitting there alone because she wants to."

Stanley brought a new board over and placed it in front of him. "Maybe the right cowboy hasn't come along ta change her mind about thangs."

Brent thought about that. No, there was too much room for conflict as far as he and Tacy were concerned.

App was watching him intently. "Yor thankin' about it. I kin tell. You should ask her out ta dinner or somethin'. I know. Take her fer a horseback ride and a picnic. Women—even

tomboy cowgirls like Tacy—enjoy picnics."
He grinned and winked at Brent. "And when
ya go, be sure and ask her about Norma Sue's
punkin chunker."

Chapter Nine

"Norma Sue, you sure this will work?" Esther Mae asked, staring at the drawing of the catapult.

"It'll work," Norma Sue snapped, looking up and glaring through her protective glasses as she prepared to use the power saw. "If I build it, it'll work. Even if we're not using any electrical triggers."

"Now, Norma," Adela cautioned in her genteel voice, causing Tacy to smile. "Don't get all worked up. Esther Mae was teasing you—weren't you, Esther?" Adela turned her serene eyes to Esther Mae.

"I'm teasing and you know it. You're just so set on beating them boys it's making you grumpy."

"Them boys are just as fixed on beating me. I heard App talking to Stanley about getting Brent to try and weasel information out of you, Tacy. So be on your guard. If he comes around asking what this chunker looks like, don't tell him anything."

"Brent's not going to get any information out of me." Tacy laughed at the idea, thinking it might be fun to see if he tried. She couldn't imagine him doing such a thing. "You really think he'd do that? I mean that they'd actually get him to do such a thing?"

Esther Mae's eyes bloomed twice their size. "Oh, yes, they would. He might even do it just to keep them from badgering you."

Norma Sue ran the saw blade through the wood in a quick, loud motion before adding, "He might even ask you out just to try and be sneaky about it."

Tacy laughed so hard her chest hurt. "Puh-leze," she wheezed. "Brent Stockwell would never ask a woman out just to see if he could find out covert information about a punkin chunker." She'd already set him straight about her dating policy, anyway.

Norma Sue's brows arched above the protective glasses. "You aren't dumb. I know you're not. But that right there was about the silliest thing I ever heard."

"I, um—I'm not sure I understand," Tacy said.

Adela patted her arm. "Norma didn't mean to sound so rude," she said, shooting her friend a sharp glance. "What she meant was that he would use it as an excuse to ask you out—you know, as a favor to the boys."

Okay, so maybe she was dumb. She still didn't understand.

Esther Mae shook her head. "Tacy, he'd ask you out because he wants to."

"Oh," she gasped. "Sorry, y'all, my mind must have been on vacation. But excuse me again for missing something here. What makes y'all so sure he'd do that? How do y'all know he wants to ask me out?" She knew he'd thought about it, but she'd been alone with him when that had happened. How did they know?

Adela looked sheepish. With her pixie cut, sparkling white hair and vivid blue eyes she was the picture of sweetness. "See, dear, I came into the diner one day through the back entrance to see my Sam. Well, I overheard Brent in the dining room talking to the three of them. They were giving him a hard time about you, and I could just tell by the way he was talking that he was interested."

"Adela can tell." Esther Mae nodded, beaming. "She always can."

Tacy didn't know what to say. Or think. There was no denying the fact that there was something between her and Brent. But she'd also set him straight. "No," she said. "I don't think he'd sink to such devious tactics."

"Believe what you will," Norma Sue said, warning in her words. "But when he asks you out, don't tell him nothing about this catapult. 'Cause it's goin' to sling a pumpkin farther than anything Applegate and his crew could ever cook up."

Tacy started to say that even if Brent asked, she wouldn't go…but then she stopped—she didn't know Brent well enough to know what he would and wouldn't do. But what bothered her was realizing that she wasn't sure what *she* would do if he decided to ignore her warning and ask her out…

"Did you sell any meat loaf today?" Brent asked her two days later when Tacy went to feed and exercise Rabbit after work. She hadn't seen him during either of the two trips she'd made to feed her horse the day before. And she'd felt strangely let down at missing him.

"Hey," she said, spinning to face him. "Where did you come from?" Where had he been?

He rested a shoulder against the stall, crossed his boots and grinned at her. The easy smile did odd things to her insides.

"I've been around. Why? Did you miss me?"

"No—" she started to say but stopped as his smile broadened. The man was gorgeous— not that it should matter to her. But it did. "How are the broncs doing?"

"Good, I've got one ready to ride and wondered if you and Rabbit might want to tag along."

It wasn't a date, but it was another chance to show him her equestrian skills and she wasn't about to pass that up. "I would be delighted."

"Did you have fun working on the catapult with Norma Sue and her gang?" he asked casually a few minutes later.

"You don't waste any time, do you?" she said.

He grinned. "I thought I'd get it out of the way. Don't you have something to ask me?"

She laughed. "Why, yes, actually, I do. How's the catapult coming?"

He chuckled and held her gaze for a long moment as they shared the inside joke. It was Tacy who broke the contact, focusing ahead as Rabbit followed the now-familiar road into the pastures. "They are taking this competition very seriously."

"You'd better believe it. You should have seen App instructing me how to saw and measure. I ran over to the lumberyard in Ranger yesterday and picked up some railroad ties for them. He decided he wanted to make it more substantial."

She shot him a smug look. "So maybe I should pass that tidbit of information along to my superiors."

"Now, c'mon. That wouldn't be right. Here I am having a nice conversation with you, and you'd betray that trust?"

She arched a brow, teasing him. "Shouldn't have volunteered it."

"Better watch out." He grinned. "I might have been giving you bad information just to foul you up."

"I figured you for a double sneak like that."

He laughed and they continued their teasing

for a while, walking the horses down the road, then along the trail. It felt strange and wonderful at the same time. Tacy was enjoying herself more than she could imagine. She was attracted to everything about Brent. His looks, the way he sat in the saddle, the patient way he worked with a horse when it wasn't totally sure about having him on its back. But she was captivated by something in his eyes most of all. Something that seemed to reach inside her every time their gazes met…maybe it was knowing the intense way he cared about the mistakes he'd made that got to her. He went much deeper than she'd first thought. Something elusive but powerful caused her pulse to grow skittish and made her feel reckless every time those serious eyes touched her— not a good thing.

"So when do you start breaking the next one?" she asked, finally catching him looking at her. In his eyes, she could see that his thoughts were heading into the same churning waters as her own.

"In the morning," he said, tension tightening his tone.

She pushed. "You know I want to help."

"No," he said immediately.

She sucked in a breath and held her temper. Temper tantrums wouldn't solve anything.... It sure was tempting, though.

Brent shifted in the saddle and the colt, feeling his rider's unease, sidestepped and fought the bit momentarily. He welcomed the distraction as he settled the animal down. He wished settling his own mood was as easy. Spending time with Tacy was dangerous. He knew this line of questioning would come up. But he hadn't been able to stop himself from asking her along. He'd missed seeing her yesterday and had found himself thinking about her all day long. It had been one of the reasons he'd timed his training of the colts when he knew she'd be working at Sam's.

"So how about that statement you made the other day?" He'd been thinking about what she'd said on Saturday, that she thought God had brought them together. "What was with that?"

She halted Rabbit and stared at him. "I believe it's true. I've been placed in your life for a reason."

"And what would that reason be?" he

asked, startled by her words, but not by her frankness. His attention was distracted by the beauty of her smile and the way her eyes twinkled warmly. He swallowed hard and found his gaze resting on those perfect lips— then forced himself to look back into her eyes, which danced with laughter. If God had sent her to distract him, then she was doing a bang-up job of it.

"That, my handsome buckaroo, is something I'm still trying to figure out. I mean, you make me mad enough to chew nails because you can't see I'm good at what I do but— Hey, I'll race you back to the corral!"

Before the exclamation was finished, she whirled Rabbit around and took off back the way they'd come. Laughing, he gave the colt the go-ahead and raced after her. Rabbit was fast and Tacy leaned low over the saddle horn and rode as if she and Rabbit were one, thundering down the path and back onto the soft road. When the colt nearly caught them, Tacy glanced over her shoulder and laughed into the rushing wind. Her eyes sparkled and his adrenaline surged as they challenged each other. Then she laughed, nudged Rabbit and sent the horse into overdrive. Instantly, the distance between them widened. Rabbit was no slouch, and neither was his rider.

Brent gave the colt a nudge and the race was on. By the time they made it back to the yard, there was no doubt about it: the girl could ride. He was pretty sure this was exactly what she wanted him to conclude.

But he wasn't thinking about that as much as he was thinking about chasing Tacy. Laughing into the wind as they went, it was the first time in two years that he'd felt a sense of joy. She was beautiful and so alive—*and driving him crazy!*

In the yard, she hopped from the saddle before Rabbit had fully stopped and stood waiting, hands on her hips, breathing heavily from the exhilaration of the chase.

He felt it, too, and swung out of the saddle, slapped the reins around the corral post and stomped toward her. She was smiling broadly, eyes sparkling with life. He wasn't thinking clearly now and he knew it. He'd never wanted to pull a woman into his arms and kiss her as much as he wanted to now—he halted a mere breath away from her, so close she had to tilt her head back to look up at him. She knew exactly what he was thinking.

"You're having fun, aren't you?" he asked, furious with the electricity crackling between them.

"Oh, yeah, cowboy," she said, placing a hand lightly against his jaw. "And I think I can help you if you let me."

His focus wavered from what she was saying because he wanted to kiss her so badly. "You can't help me—" he said, and before he could stop himself he lowered his head and pressed his lips to hers. His hands wrapped about her arms and he tugged her close. He expected her to pull away—maybe slap him even, but she didn't. She felt right in his arms, her lips felt right against his as she returned his kiss. Regaining some semblance of sanity, knowing he wasn't feeling rational, Brent pulled back. He was not the careless idiot he'd been two years before. This was too important—Tacy was too important—for him to go too fast.

He rested his forehead against hers, his fingers tightening against her back. This was crazy. There were so many reasons he shouldn't let this happen. But oh how he wanted it, wanted her.

"I really do think I'm here to help you," she said softly, breathlessly. "I'm not Tina."

Pulling back, she looked up and held his gaze. "Our names both start with *T* but other than that we are not the same. I'm an expert when it comes to riding and understanding the feel of a horse. All I'm asking you for is professional guidance as I try a breaking technique I've been studying for months. I'm going to step into the stirrup of an unbroken horse with or without your help. What I'm asking you for is assurance that I've done my homework when I put my boot into that stirrup."

He dropped his hands and stepped away.

"I'm not judging Tina, because I don't know her reasons for wanting to get on that horse—but for me this is no game. I can do this. You have blinders on, and it's not good. Not good for you or me."

"Not happening," he said tersely. What had he been thinking, letting his head get messed around? That kiss wasn't her caring about him. It was all about her getting her way. About her getting on the back of one of those horses.

"Teaching me could help you get over your phobia. And it could be fun."

"No, Tacy."

Her expression tensed. "You are so stubborn."

"Yeah, I am. I have good reason to be. We went over this already."

She took hold of Rabbit's reins and stormed inside the barn.

Birdy lifted her head from where she'd been watching them and thumped her tail. She looked as if she knew he was a mixed-up man. "You're exactly right. She makes me crazy," Brent growled, spun on his heel and strode back to the corral.

The man was making her crazy!

Tacy had to force herself to calm down as she removed Rabbit's saddle, not wanting to scare or hurt the poor horse. But boy, she sure would like to wring Brent's neck.

Her lips still tingled from his kiss. The kiss had been perfect...but a kiss was not going to help her face facts. *Oh, no.* That kiss was just going to confuse the issue all the more.

Easier said than done. She had never, ever been kissed like that before and somehow it seemed like so much more than just a kiss. *"Enough,"* she growled at herself, grabbing a brush and pulling it along Rabbit's coat.

"He probably thinks I'm a blooming idiot—" she said, looking Rabbit in the eye as her hand trembled.

She flirted, teased and generally enjoyed giving guys a hard time. She was *always* in control as far as men were concerned. But she'd felt totally out of control just now—and several other times she had been with Brent. There was something between them that was undeniable.

Frankly it scared her. It would only complicate things.

Right!

After all, she didn't want to get involved with any guy right now.

She had plans. Goals that had to be achieved, or at least set into motion, before she allowed her heart to get distracted with… with—men. *Right!*

She *would* keep her head on straight.

She *would* keep her eye on her goals—she wanted to break horses. And she would.

But… She stopped brushing and stared into the grazing area outside Rabbit's stall. She also wanted to see that hollow look disappear from Brent's eyes when he talked about his family. She couldn't deny it.

Drat! And double *drat!* Things were really mingling and mangling inside her head, and she wasn't sure at all what to do about it.

Goals or no goals, she was falling for the handsome, haunted cowboy.

Chapter Ten

Brent had been in a foul mood for the last three days and as he loaded feed into the back of his truck at Pete's Feed and Seed not even the happy color of the canary-yellow building was helping. Especially since he'd seen Tacy enter the salon across the street as he'd gone into the feed store. Knowing she was over there only upped his irritation at himself. He'd kissed her, and now he couldn't stop thinking about it. Or the fact that he was a darn fool—the words of his dad rang in his head.

He looked up from his work when Pete came out of the store. A large man with a balding head and an easy manner, Pete crossed his arms over his oversize chest and smiled. "How's the horses comin' along?"

"Good." Brent was glad he'd asked about the animals and nothing more.

A truck pulled into a parking space across the street and Norma Sue climbed out. The heavyset ranch woman wore blue overalls and a red, long-sleeved shirt, and on her head sat a red cowboy hat. Her wiry gray curls stuck out from under the brim. If it had been white hair, like Adela's, Norma would have looked like a Texas Mrs. Claus. Then again, he guessed she still did, even without the snow-white hair.

Even in his bad mood he couldn't help but wave back at the jovial woman when she lifted her hand in greeting. She started to step up onto the sidewalk, heading to the salon, when she suddenly spun around and headed his way.

"Heads up," Pete warned. "You are on the radar."

"Maybe it's you, not me." Brent grabbed a sack of feed and tossed it onto the others in the truck.

"Nope. You're the one helping App and Stanley build that punkin chunker. She's been asking everyone she sees what it looks like, so I'm pretty sure you're the one she's comin' ta see. Afternoon, Norma," he greeted as she crossed the yellow line in the road.

"Same to you, Pete. It's a nice one, that's for sure. How are you today, Brent?"

Brent grabbed the next bag, noting that he had four to go. "I'm fine, Norma Sue. How are you?"

"Fine. Just fine. So, is y'all's chunker finished yet?"

Pete was standing off to the side of Norma Sue, so she couldn't see his face as he raised his brows at Brent and grinned real big. Brent started to answer when he heard what sounded like a herd of cattle rumbling along the sidewalk behind him. Norma Sue's eyes widened, and he turned to see Applegate and Stanley thundering toward them.

"Norma Sue," Applegate boomed as he came to a halt. "Sam said Adela said y'all got yer machine almost ready to test."

"Well, why would she go and tell him a thing like that?"

"Maybe," Stanley drawled, situating his bag of sunflower seeds more securely in the crook of his arm, "because he's her husband."

Brent glanced across toward the salon and saw Lacy and Tacy watching from the window. He could see them grinning even from this distance.

"Well, I was just asking Brent here if y'all got yours ready to test."

Brent shot her a look but was smart enough to keep his mouth shut. He didn't want to get in the middle of this. He had horses to train and other more important things on his mind.

"You didn't tell her nothin', did you?" App asked, sharp eyes squinting at the cowboy.

Brent scowled. "No. But I'm not sure I see why it would hurt anything to admit it."

"Oh, so you admit that it's finished." Norma Sue beamed triumphantly while Applegate and Stanley scowled like he was a traitor.

"Well, no, ma'am, I didn't say that—"

"Yes, you did," she said. "So when are y'all testing it?"

"You didn't have to go and tell our secrets," App accused. "We got you on this team 'cause we thought you could keep yer mouth shut."

"Yeah, that's right," Stanley agreed, spitting a sunflower seed at Brent's feet.

Pete chuckled. Brent glared at him. This was getting entirely out of hand. "What is the big deal?" he snapped. "And for the record, I said no such thing."

"It don't rightly matter," App said. "Cat's out of the bag now."

Brent grabbed two bags of feed and tossed them into the truck. "Look, I thought this was a friendly competition."

"Well, it is," Norma Sue said. "Whatever gave you the idea it wasn't?"

Huh? He looked from her to his team-mates. "Are you telling me *this* is friendly?"

Stanley scratched his bald spot and grinned. "We tend to get a bit carried away."

Brent tossed his last two bags of feed into the truck. "Yeah, you do."

They all stared at him. "What?" he asked, feeling ill-tempered.

"Are you mad?" Norma Sue asked.

"Ain't no call to be mad," Applegate said.

"Shore not," Stanley agreed and tossed a few more seeds into his mouth. "We's jest havin' some fun."

"Fun?" Brent said and found himself staring at the salon with anger in his eyes. Maybe if Tacy didn't have him all tied in knots he'd see some humor in all this, but as it was he wasn't laughing yet. He yanked open his truck door and climbed in.

"You comin' to the Thanksgiving dinner at

church?" Norma Sue asked, walking over to stand by his window. "It might help you get over your bad temper."

At this point he wasn't sure anything would help. "Fine, I'll be there," he said, feeling a touch of remorse at having lost his temper.

She gave him a wide grin and tipped her red hat at him. "Good. You take care now."

What had just happened? Here he thought he was going to have to step in and stop a real fight, and he'd ended up agreeing to attend Thanksgiving dinner with all of them. The townsfolk of Mule Hollow were certainly strange. Strange, but nice, he had to admit.

"They've got him so turned around he doesn't know which way is up and which way is down," Lacy Matlock said, laughing, from the window of her salon. "Poor cowboy."

Tacy couldn't help feeling sorry for Brent. From what Lacy had told her, this so-called feud between Applegate and Norma Sue was just the two of them having a little fun. She had to admit she had thought they were genuinely furious at each other, too. "You mean to tell me they aren't really at each other's throats?"

Lacy led Tacy back to the cutting chair so Lacy could finish her haircut.

"Oh, they're perturbed at each other, and each is bound and determined to beat the other. But they're having fun. They're just competitive."

"Brent looked as if he thought they were about to try to kill each other."

Lacy chuckled. "Yes, he did. So how's it going with you two out at the ranch?"

"Not so good. What was Sheri thinking? I mean, I came here so Pace could teach me, and then he leaves and sends in his place a rodeo star who would rope and hog-tie me before he'd let me on the back of an unbroken colt."

Lacy slid the hot-pink comb through a section of hair, then combed it straight up and held it between her fingers. "Well, I don't really like to talk, but I'm going to let you in on something because I feel like you have a right to know."

"Anything you can tell me that would help me understand what this is all about would be great."

"Pace was worried about Brent. You see, when he took the job out there in Idaho, he was angry about something that had happened in his life. Family issues."

"Yes, I know that."

Lacy grinned. "He told you."

Tacy hesitated at Lacy's obvious excitement. "Yes," she said cautiously.

"Great, then they were right."

"They were right about what?"

Lacy waved the scissors. "No, hang on. I'm getting ahead of myself, but I was just so excited to hear that he opened up to you. This is good. Very, very good. Anyway," she said, snipping off the tips of the hair sticking up between her fingers, "you see, Pace says the Great Basin is such a vast space that a man can tend to his work and have almost no contact with anyone all year long if he wants it that way. Pace worked out there because he loved it. He is such a throwback to the old West cowboy that, for him, it was a love affair with the land and the life. For Brent it was a different story. Brent was running away from something. He wasn't there because he loved it, but to punish himself. Pace told Sheri that just wasn't right. Ever since Pace moved here, he said the Lord kept putting Brent in his mind."

Tacy met her gaze in the mirror. She agreed

with Pace's assessment of Brent. The man had been hurting and guilt-ridden. He'd been punishing himself.

"So when Pace had to leave unexpectedly, Brent was the first person he thought of…said he realized it was a good time to see if he could draw Brent back into the real world."

"Even if it meant messing up my plans," Tacy said, but there was no anger in her words.

Lacy snipped. "Actually, Sheri was the one who messed with your plans. See, Pace wanted to call and let you in on everything, knowing you'd probably go somewhere else to break horses."

Tacy met Lacy's blue eyes in the mirror. "Sheri wanted me here." It wasn't a question but a statement. Sheri had acted evasive over the phone when she'd called her that first day after meeting Brent. "But why?"

Lacy dipped her chin and a blond curl fell across one eye as she gave Tacy a Duh-think-about-it stare. "She thought getting the two of us to butt heads would help?"

"Is it working?" Lacy asked, instead of denying anything.

Tacy thought of the kiss they'd shared three days earlier. She'd been in a funk ever since that kiss. Even the customers at Sam's had noticed. Poor Jess had stopped flirting with her after she'd practically growled at him.

"Honestly, Lacy. He confided in me because he felt that since he wasn't letting me in the arena I deserved to know why he was so against it." She didn't elaborate because it wasn't her right to tell, and she knew Lacy totally understood that. "He was right to tell me. I get why he's against it, so I've backed off. I mean, he's hurting about something and me pushing to get in with those horses is only making things worse. But I do feel like I'm here for a reason. It's kind of a weird feeling. I think I'm here to help him, but I don't have a clue how to do that." She didn't mention that she was also so attracted to him that she couldn't think straight. She really didn't enjoy feeling so out of her element.

Finished with the cut, Lacy combed all of Tacy's hair down and picked up her blow dryer and brush. "Maybe you're here to push him."

"No, you don't understand. When I push, fireworks happen."

Lacy pointed the blow-dryer at her in the mirror like a gun. "You are not the kind of woman who is scared of fireworks. Jump in there and let them fly. The smoke will clear eventually." She smiled impishly.

"But—"

"No buts. Did you ever stop and think that maybe he needs some fireworks? There is nothing like tension to make a man face the truth."

Tacy's mouth dropped open and her heart did a free fall. Could Lacy be right? "But what if we're wrong?"

"What if we're right?" Lacy countered with a big smile.

Chapter Eleven

When Tacy got back to Pace and Sheri's, Birdy was snuggled up in her bed beside the door—with Brent's boot.

"How are you feeling, you little thief?" she asked, bending down to pet her friend and make sure she was okay. She was going to have to keep a close watch on her because she was due any day now. Snuggling with Brent's boot might be a sign that the time was near. She was obviously nesting.

"I really hate to take the boot away from you, sugar, but I'm going to have to." She was also going to have to tell Brent to stop tempting the poor dog by leaving his boots outside. Thank goodness he had two pairs he worked in or else he'd be up a creek.

After changing into her riding clothes, Tacy drove to Brent's and set his boot on the porch beside the other one. She could see him in the corral working one of the colts. As she caught sight of him he was preparing to place a horse blanket on a colt's back for what was obviously the first time. She headed that way, watching and listening. The colt wasn't sure about the whole idea, but Brent was speaking to it calmly. His voice was wonderfully reassuring. The baritone rumble of it was so enticing that Tacy was certain it would calm anything and anyone he spoke to—she herself could listen to it all day long.

There she went getting sidetracked again. Striding to the corral, she climbed to the top of the board, threw her legs over and took a seat. Seeing her, the colt jumped sideways, which won her an instant scowl from Brent. He *really* needed to get over that scowling or his face might just freeze that way. It dawned on her that his heart might be in danger of the same thing.

Shooting him a grin, she crossed her arms and sat perfectly still. He was grinding his molars so hard the poor man was going to have TMJ before the sun went down. "Get back to work." She mouthed the words silently. He turned away from her, and she couldn't help smiling. He knew as well as she did that the horse would accept her after a few minutes if she was still and quiet. Brent, however, was an entirely different ball game. He glared again, then turned back to the horse, evidently determined to ignore her.

Which was fine with Tacy as long as she got to observe him now. She loved watching him work. He was patient as the day was long—with a horse. Teaching a horse to trust you was an art. You had to get the animal to realize you meant no harm. Anytime you earned an animal's trust, it was better all the way around. Horses were just like people in that respect.

She wondered how she could earn Brent's trust. In a way, he'd already shown that he trusted her by confiding his past. Forcing the issue of breaking horses might ruin that and she knew it.

But, as Lacy had pointed out, it also might help him. Sitting there watching him work the colt while he ignored her, Tacy closed her eyes and prayed that God would lead her. That He would help her know how to handle this situation. She also prayed that He would forgive her if she messed up. She was afraid of messing up…but then she was just going to have to trust God to fix her goofs if they weren't part of the big plan.

After about an hour, Brent tied the horse and stalked her way. Watching him, she had a flashback of the last time he walked purposefully toward her like that—she forced the kiss out of her mind and climbed from the top of the corral.

"You're bothering the horse by being here," he said, opening the gate and walking out.

She scooted out behind him. "You know as well as I do that it forgot about me after a few minutes."

His glare hit her like a brick as he shook his head in disgust or frustration before stomping toward the cabin.

"You are so stubborn, Brent. I only brought your boot back, if you really want to know why I'm here," she called, hurrying behind him. "You might want to keep it inside. Birdy was treating it like a puppy this morning."

She saw his lip twitch and knew he thought that was cute. The man had a soft spot for her dog.

"Has she had pups before?" he asked, stopping at the steps. He wore buckskin chaps over faded jeans and a button-down, long-sleeved shirt—she dragged her mind away from thinking how rugged and *safe* he looked. She forced herself not to think about how wonderful it had felt to be held in those strong arms.

She took a deep breath and shook her head. "First litter, but the vet says she should be fine. Her mother always had good luck delivering pups, so I don't anticipate a problem."

"Good."

He stepped up onto the porch and headed toward the door without saying anything else. She'd expected an argument, even a fight. She hadn't expected to be totally dismissed. Okay, so he'd said a few words, but how could he just go into the cabin and leave her standing there?

Spinning around, Tacy stomped back to the barn and fed Rabbit. When she was done she waited, toe tapping beside the corral, but Brent didn't return. She checked her watch. An hour had passed.

This was ridiculous. She glared at the cabin and imagined him sitting in there, watching her. She crossed her arms, jutted a hip forward and fumed. The horse Brent had been working snorted, and she glanced toward it, furious when she saw it calmly waiting for him.

Was Brent playing her? Trying to manipulate her? Did he think that if he went inside all he'd have to do was wait until she gave up and left? *Ha!* She'd get him out of there if he was watching. Instead of heading toward her truck, she went straight toward the corral. With a glance over her shoulder at the front window of the cabin, she opened the gate and slipped inside with the colt. Two could play this game.

She wasn't as easily manipulated as he thought she was, and thanks to Lacy, she was seeing things in a whole new light.

What was the beautiful little fool doing?

Brent was out the door and down the steps the instant he realized Tacy was going into the pen. She was supposed to go home. She wasn't supposed to go in with the colt. At least it was tied up and the other colts were in a different pen.

The moment he entered the corral he

realized he'd been had. Tacy wasn't down at the end of the corral with the colt.

She was leaning against the chute waiting for him.

"Hey, cowboy, about time you showed up."

His gaze narrowed and his temper flared. "What are you doing?"

"Waiting for you, honey bunch," she said with an exaggerated smile as she held her wrist up so the face of her watch was toward him. "You made great time. Four seconds flat from the moment I unhooked that latch. You must have had your nose stuck to the corner of that window, watching like a hawk, expecting me to just lope over to my truck and leave lickety-split."

"Okay, so you got me. Now you want to come out of there?"

"Nope. I don't think so. I think I belong here. Look, he's not complaining." She studied the colt, then turned uncompromising eyes toward him. "I wasn't sure how to handle this. After you told me about your sister, I backed off because I respect your feelings and understand that you're hurting inside and feeling guilty about what happened with her and the horse."

"Come out," he said sternly, not at all pleased with the turn of conversation.

She planted her feet. "As I said, I'm staying." She crossed her arms and challenged him with her stare.

The woman looked entirely too cute with that smug, defiant glint in her eyes. "Tacy, don't push me," he growled. She shook her head and took a step away from him. He moved toward her. "I'm warning you."

Her mouth fell open then, and she looked amazingly playful. "Or what? Are you going to throw me over your shoulder and carry me out of here?"

"Don't tempt me." Instead of looking the least bit worried, she tilted her head back and laughed! "Hey, I'll do it," he warned, taking another step toward her, making his spurs clink.

Uncertainty clouded her eyes. "Don't be silly. I was just joking."

"I'm not." He called her bluff and took another step closer. She backed up, glancing at the colt watching them.

"You're scaring the colt."

"Obviously, he's not too worried about you. He looks fine to me."

Her eyes lit up as she stuffed her fists into her pockets. "Noticed that, have you."

"Noticed what?"

"That the horse isn't too worried about me being in here. I was wondering if you'd admit it. There, you have."

He stared from her to the colt. It was true that it didn't look too worried about her being here. And he'd already admitted that she did have a way with animals. "Have you always been so pigheaded?"

"Always."

They had a staring showdown, and he was really tempted to actually snatch her up and carry her out the gate—but he knew that would frighten the colt in the process, undoing the work he'd already done. He studied Tacy.

"You don't have a comeback?" she asked.

"Honestly, no. You confuse me."

"Hey, I'm an open book," she said, then climbed back up to her perch on the top board of the corral. She chuckled when she looked down at him. The colt snickered right along with her. "Besides, confusing is good." She patted the board beside her. "Climb on up here and take a load off. Ask me anything. I think we need to talk and get some of this confusion cleared up."

The last thing he wanted to do was sit beside her and let her try to whittle down his resolve. But what could he do? He climbed up beside her anyway…so close their knees touched.

"Don't look so glum—we're just talking," she said. "It looked like you got sandwiched between App and Norma this afternoon."

"You looked like you were enjoying the show," he grumbled.

"I will admit it was fun watching. You weren't sure if they were about to duke it out or not." She chuckled and nudged him with her shoulder. "Admit it. You were scared you were about to have to referee."

He laughed. "Okay, you're right. I didn't know what was happening."

"Believe me, they're just having a good time, despite the look of things. Lacy said they're always finding something to stir up mischief between them."

He found himself losing his train of thought as he watched her dancing eyes. Suddenly, the green in them darkened, catching him off guard. Just as unexpectedly, she touched his arm, squeezing it gently.

"Are you going home for Thanksgiving?" she asked quietly.

They'd gone from frustrated to teasing to serious business in seconds. How did she do that to him? "No, I'm not," he said firmly. He wished she'd stop it. His mother's disappointed voice now rang in his ears.

"I bet your mom didn't like that when you told her."

He didn't want to talk about this, but her concern got to him. "She was disappointed," he admitted and tried not to think about how much sadness he'd heard in her voice when they'd last spoken. "But it's for the best."

"It would be good for you to go home and stop running."

He grimaced. "Is that what you think? That I'm running?" Instead of giving him a quick comeback, her eyes darkened even further.

"Yes, actually. I know it's not my business, but from what you told me I can't help feeling that you must go home."

He straightened, his shoulders suddenly feeling knotted up. "Tacy, you have no idea—"

"You know what they say about getting back on a horse after you've been thrown…"

"That has nothing to do with this."

"But it does, Brent. You made a mistake. A really tragic mistake. But your sister is doing better, praise the Lord. And you've learned from what happened. You know what I think is the saddest thing about all this? The fact that it has come between you and your dad. I'm sure that's hurting your mom something terrible."

Brent looked away. "You're right. This isn't your business." Yup, he was being a jerk. No doubt about it.

She knocked him in the knee with her knee. "Hey, we might not be friends, exactly, but we're neighbors and neighbors care about neighbors."

"Or they're just being plain nosy."

She let out an I-don't-care laugh. "If you think being mean is scaring me, you're wrong."

"This is insane. Is there something in the water around here that makes people—"

"Care?"

"*Not* the word I was looking for. More like ornery busybodies."

She chuckled. "If there is, then you've been guzzling *way* too much of it."

His concentration was shot to smithereens as her snappy words hit him. His lips twitched against his will, and before he could help it he smiled.

"Oh!" she exclaimed and threw a hand to her heart. "The cowboy doth smile."

"Funny."

"*No*, really, you should do it more often. It's nice. Really nice," she said with a warmth that shot straight to his heart and set it racing.

She wasn't being sassy, just genuinely nice. On the one hand, looking at her, being near her, made him want to smile. On the other hand, she aggravated him no end. He was totally falling for Tacy Jones and he knew it. Needing to put distance between them, he hopped down from the fence. Determined not to help him at all, she followed. And wasn't it just his luck that she landed with a thud and a grunt as her ankle turned. Immediately, he grabbed her arm to steady her and just like that found himself too close again for comfort.

"Oops," she said, as breathless as he suddenly felt.

"Are you okay?" he managed to ask. The woman had the biggest eyes—looking into them was just plain dangerous.

She inhaled slowly before answering.

"Just checking your reflexes. Now about that horse—don't you think you could give a girl a chance?"

The *horse*. Here he was thinking about Tacy and all she was thinking about was that darn colt and how to get him to let her break it!

Some fool he was. He dropped his hand from her arm and pointed at the gate. "Out, Tacy. Now!"

Chapter Twelve

"Stop with the commands," Tacy said the second she was out of the corral. "I'm trying to help. You have a problem. You realize that, don't you?"

"*You* are my problem. I'm trying to protect you, and all you want to do is—"

"Is what *I* want to do. Yes, I know. And you don't have any reason to keep me from doing that. I'm not a child or a teenager. I'm a grown, capable woman and you can't tell me you haven't noticed that."

He started to say something, but instead slammed his mouth into a tight line as his gaze slid over her. She crossed her arms and stared up at him. She remembered every detail of his kiss. What in the world was she thinking when she even toyed with the idea that he was someone she could fall in love with? The very thought was ridiculous. Still, her mind kept coming back to that thought time and again. *Ridiculous!* "Well, are you going to just stand there? Haven't you noticed that I'm a capable woman?"

His eyes narrowed to match hers. "Oh, I've noticed that you're a woman, all right. No denying that." He stepped closer now, invading her space. "A beautiful, feisty woman who likes to get her way. Even if she has to manipulate men to get it."

He thinks I'm beautiful! She smiled like a goofball at him and tried to keep her thoughts straight—easier said than done. She was enjoying his nearness more than she wanted or needed to. "My way is the way it was supposed to be in the first place," she said, forcing herself to focus on what was pertinent to her goals. "Come on, Brent. You have a problem and I'm the solution. You need help out here. You need help riding these horses in order to get enough time in the saddle on them before the owners pick them up. You need me." It was absolutely true, and he knew it. Either he was going to have to let her help or hire someone else.

They stared at each other, locked in a battle of wills. No doubt he would see the light. The man was smart. Surely his common sense would kick in and he would realize this was different from when he'd allowed his sister to climb up on the back of an unbroken horse.

After a tension-filled moment, he stepped back. "What I do with the colts is not your concern. You aren't—"

That did it! "You are a real piece of work, cowboy," she snapped, taking a step toward him, invading his space this time. "Here I thought you had a brain and maybe a heart, but you're just closed-minded and selfish!" Turning away, she stalked toward her truck but spun back to face him again. "I can ride those colts. And even if I were to get on one and get thrown on my backside, it would be better than being too afraid to give it a go. You know what you are, Brent Stockwell? You're a chauvinistic chicken!"

She stormed to her truck and fumed all the way home. She felt childish and validated at the same time. She didn't like anything about this. Not one single thing.

* * *

Despite his foul mood, Brent stayed after church the next day because Norma Sue wouldn't hear of him leaving. They were eating and then playing volleyball—and she was determined to get Brent to participate.

He'd never seen so much food in all his life, but Applegate assured him that come next week at the churchwide Thanksgiving dinner, there'd be twice the food. Brent probably wouldn't see that spread, but he didn't tell App. Instead, he piled his plate full, carried it over to a table and sat down. His gaze drifted across the fellowship hall to the table where Tacy sat with a group of women around her age. She was laughing, and hearing it made his stomach roll over like the first time he stuck his boot in the stirrup of a rodeo bronc. He'd instinctively known what to do with that bronc.... He didn't have a clue what to do with Tacy, and it was driving him crazy.

Unlike him, she seemed to be having a great time today. When she'd left his house the day before, she hadn't been happy—oh, no, the redheaded troublemaker had been hotter than a firecracker on the Fourth of July.

And despite everything—every harsh word he'd said to her—it had bothered him all night long. She was under the wrong assumption that he enjoyed denying her something she wanted so much. She had no idea what havoc she was causing within him.

Seeing her happy now gave him pause. Was everything about their relationship—what little they had and however odd it might be—purely a ruse to get on a horse's back? The thought plagued him like a nail in his boot. He understood perfectly that it bothered him because he wanted her to feel something for him that went far beyond getting her way.

As if feeling his eyes upon her, Tacy looked his way and held his gaze for a second. A second that stilled his heartbeat and stole his breath.

He was floundering, and he knew it.

He was supposed to be training horses, and all he could think about was a green-eyed gal with copper-colored hair and a fiery determination that drew him like a flame. Tacy Jones was becoming important to him, no matter how much he tried to deny it.

"She's a complex piece of work, isn't she?"

Brent pulled his head out of the clouds and

stared at the cowboy who'd just taken the chair beside him. It was Jess.

Brent stared at him, not sure how he was supposed to answer. He kept his mouth shut so Jess could clarify it on his own. At Brent's hard stare, the cowboy glanced toward Tacy and shrugged.

"I'm just saying she's a puzzle. I can't figure her out, though I'm trying my best. You're looking at her like you'd like to—" He paused.

Brent's mood went south with that pause. "To what?" he asked, the edge to his voice as sharp as the way his temper had spiked.

Jess's brows dipped. "Hey, nothing bad implied here, so back down, man. All I'm saying is, you look like you want to get to know her, too. She's great. Who wouldn't want to be the guy to get past that barrier she's put up to block us out?"

Brent's temp backed off a few degrees. Maybe he'd jumped to conclusions he shouldn't have, but the thought of this cowboy or any other even thinking about Tacy didn't sit well with him. Not caring to continue the conversation with Jess, he picked up a forkful of stuffing and rammed it into his mouth.

Brent knew he was attracted to Tacy on a physical level, but it went deeper than that. She had this uncanny way of knowing what he was thinking—that irritated and intrigued him at the same time. It got him to thinking about things. How did she do that? Like her telling him he needed to go home for Thanksgiving. Tacy had picked up on that instantly.

His mom's reaction pricked his conscience. It wasn't her fault he'd chosen the wrong path—the way of booze and women—when he'd had everything going for him. It wasn't her fault he'd let his wilder side kick in rather than sticking with the good upbringing he'd been given. It was something he would regret for the rest of his life—and not something he wanted to think about right now. He pushed aside those thoughts and concentrated on the food on his plate. He was staring at his sweet potatoes when Jess elbowed him in the side.

"Seems like one of us is ahead in the game."

Brent glared at him. "What are you talking about?"

The cowboy jerked his head in Tacy's direction. "She keeps stealing glances this way and, sadly, it's not me she's looking at.

Matter of fact, I don't even think she's noticed I'm sitting here beside you."

Brent slid his gaze Tacy's way. Sure enough, she shot him a quick, penetrating glance. Her eyes were clear as a green flame and he felt the burn all the way across the room. It left no doubt that she was just as mad at him today as she'd been yesterday.

"Nothing new there," he said to Jess. "She's just mad at me. Again."

"Hey, don't sell that short. At least that's got her attention. Don't get me wrong. I'm a big fan of the sassy side of her, but that glare you just got—well, that's one hundred percent, pure-grade emotion right there. That's priceless." Jess stood and grabbed his plate. "I wouldn't waste it if I were you."

Jess's observation was not lost on Brent. Still, the cowboy had no idea what kind of eggshells he and Tacy were treading on. He looked her way again, but she'd gathered her plate and glass and was telling everyone goodbye. He watched her walk to the trash and head out the door. He couldn't pull his eyes from her.

He had a problem. What he wanted to do about this unexpected complication was the question he had yet to answer.

* * *

"Birdy, where are you?" Tacy walked into the barn and wasn't greeted by the familiar bark. Rabbit, though, poked his head over the stall gate and gave her a welcoming snort.

She paused in her search to gently scratch him between the eyes. "Hey, boy, how's it going? Have you seen our little mama-to-be today?"

The horse pawed the ground and batted his big eyes at her.

"Too bad I can't understand that answer," Tacy said, continuing on to peek into the other stalls. They were empty. Anxiety was slowly creeping into her mind. She should have stayed home from church this morning. Birdy had been wearing a look that said today was the day. Not being able to find the expectant mother now had her worried. If she hadn't been so concerned, she'd have been glad for the distraction from her convoluted thoughts about Brent.

"Birdy, come on, girl, where are you?" she called as she walked across the yard toward Brent's cabin. She wanted to find her blue-heeler and get her home before Brent showed up. That had been part of the reason she left the lunch early. She was worried about Birdy, but also if she'd stayed any longer she might have gone over to Brent and made a fool of herself in front of the entire church congregation.

The sound of a truck gave her a sinking feeling just before Brent drove around the curve and came over the cattle guard. She should have known he'd leave the volleyball game early. She'd kinda hoped Norma Sue would trap him on the sand and not let him go. But, no, the man just couldn't help but find new ways to mess up her life.

Her knees felt shaky as he got out of his truck. "I'm looking for Birdy," she said more hastily than she'd intended. "Did you see her before you left for church this morning?"

"I saw her head into the barn. Did you look there?"

"Yes. I was about to look behind the cabin. I'm thinking she's ready to give birth, and now I'm worried because I just assumed she'd have her babies in her bed. I put soft towels in there for her and everything."

"Let me help. She might have decided to hide under the house. When I was growing up, we had a dog that had several litters of pups under the shed."

"I can do it on my own," Tacy said, heading

toward the side of the small cabin and crouching down to stare under the dark building.

Brent dropped down beside her. "Good thing about the cabin is the blocks aren't too low to the ground."

She stared at him. Had he not heard a word she'd just said? "Really, Brent, I've got this. You probably have horses to ride." Okay, so she was cranky. Sue her.

He pulled his head out from under the house and met her glare with dancing, teasing eyes. "What I'm going to *do* is go get a flashlight."

Fuming, she watched him stand and saunter off. She didn't want his help. She was half-afraid of her crazy self—the one who kept thinking about the kiss they'd shared. The same side of herself that kept tossing around images of the two of them growing old together. Crazy, crazy, crazy.

Them as a married couple. Ha! They wouldn't last a month.

"Birdy, are you under here, girl?" she called, more than anxious to find the missing dog and get the show on the road back to her place. The cabin wasn't that large, but she couldn't make out anything in the murky darkness.

"See anything?"

She jumped at the sound of Brent's voice so close. "Don't do that! You scared me!" she exclaimed.

He grinned and dropped down beside her. "Sorry. I didn't mean to."

"Oh, try that one on someone who doesn't know you, mister."

"So you admit it." He laughed, sending little jolts spinning across her skin.

"Admit what?"

"That you know me."

She sat back on her haunches. "Well, in a manner of speaking. You *are* my neighbor. We *have* argued a lot."

He leaned forward on his knees, his eyes dropping to her lips. "Yep. We've argued, all right. Kind of fun, isn't it?"

Tacy's heart was pounding out of control. Just another couple of inches and they could be kissing again— Whoa! What was she thinking? She slammed a shaky hand down on his shoulder. "Back up, cowboy. I don't think we're on the same page here."

His gaze lifted to hers. "Oh, I think we are and you know it."

The chemistry sparked between them like a grass fire in July. "W-w-well," she managed, having to swallow hard because her throat had gone dust-bowl dry. "Wha-what I do know is that Birdy needs us to find her." There, she'd managed to turn the conversation back on target. Not an easy thing to do when all she was thinking about was the feel of his lips on hers.

Brent was a fool. He knew it, but that wasn't stopping him from pushing Tacy. He was losing it because if she was smart—and she was—then she'd take his obvious attraction to her and use it against him to get what she wanted. It was a very slippery slope he was treading on.

Yanking his head out of the clouds, he bent and shone the light under the dark house. "She's not on this side," he said, feeling Tacy's shoulder against his as she leaned forward to look. He kept his gaze straight ahead and told himself to stop pushing the issue of their attraction. "Let's go around to the other side." He hopped up and headed that way without waiting for her to respond. Putting distance between them was a smart move.

"Do you think there's another place she would have gone?" Tacy asked at his elbow.

"Did you check that shed in the woods between your place and mine?"

There was a trail that ran through the woods between the two spreads but Tacy always drove to the cabin and never walked through the woods. The old shed hadn't crossed her mind. "No, I didn't think about it. Let's look on this side and then head out there."

He nodded, hiding a smile. She'd just taken charge. Gone was the vulnerable woman he'd glimpsed a minute before when she was clearly torn over her attraction to him. This Tacy was the one who would do whatever she needed to get him to let her break a horse. The thought gnawed at him as he led the way to the other side of the house: could he keep standing up to her when he was also falling so hard for her?

He figured he would owe Birdy dog treats from here 'til her pups were grown and gone for giving him this excuse to spend time with her without fighting. But he was under no illusion that things between him and Tacy would ever run smoothly.

Chapter Thirteen

"There you are," Tacy said, staring into the dark corner under the shed where Birdy had chosen to hide. It was too dark to count all the pups, but from what she could tell by the beam of the flashlight it looked like about five.

"She definitely chose to have her babies in seclusion," Brent said.

He was leaning down beside Tacy, and they were sharing space gazing beneath the shed. Tacy pulled back and sank to the ground next to him. "What next? Should I crawl under there and pull them out?" She hated tight spaces, but if she had to do it she would.

He rose to one knee and crossed his wrist on top of it, letting the flashlight dangle. "No, if there is any crawling to be done, I'll do it.

I'm just thinking it might be easier if I go grab a shovel and dig in from the side. If I don't, this old building is so close to the ground I might get stuck and you'd leave me there." He grinned at her and lifted his brows.

Tacy bit back a smile. "Now, why would you think I'd do something like that? Payback, maybe?"

"I've been on the receiving end of your meat-loaf offer, that's why."

She laughed at that. "You were *so* easy."

"You looked too innocent. I never suspected you'd do something so devious."

"Hey, a girl's got to have some fun sometimes." She matched his smile with one of her own and for a moment the tension between them dissipated. They were like an on/off switch, Tacy thought. It felt nice, though. More than nice—it felt hopeful. *Hopeful of what?* The question brought her up short. "You need to grab that shovel," she said, drawing back from the brink of letting her guard down with him. She'd done that too many times, only to have him be more than uncooperative. It wasn't happening again. The man would be bossing her around and telling her no within the hour, no doubt. There were only two things she and Brent Stockwell could do well—argue…and tease. Okay, three. But she definitely wasn't going there…

"You sure are lost in thought," Brent drawled, giving her a half grin that made him look as dashing as George Clooney in a cowboy hat.

Tacy reeled in her runaway thoughts, giving him a stern stare. "The shovel," she said, pointing in the direction of the barn.

His half grin bloomed into a full-blown, knee-knocker of a smile. "You were thinking about me, weren't you?"

"Don't get your hopes up. Now are you going to grab that shovel or am I?"

He laughed, and then, to her total and as-tounded amazement, reached out and tapped her on the nose.

"I'll be back. Don't go anywhere."

She watched him jog away through the woods and sighed long and slow. What was it between them? They'd been so ticked at each other yesterday that she shouldn't have given him the time of day today. What was she doing? Why she was flirting with him like a great second date?

She was still wondering a few minutes

later when Brent came back with a shovel and a box lined with a towel.

"I thought we might need this," he said, handing the box to her. "Miss me?"

"Like a migraine."

He grinned and strode past her. "Yep, you missed me," he said, then rounded the corner out of sight.

Instead of following him, she dropped to her stomach and started talking to Birdy, who was a bit unnerved about the sounds the shovel made as Brent went to work.

"How's our little mama doing?" Brent called from around the corner.

"Same as me. Not too happy with you right now. I think she feels threatened. My girl is smarting up about you finally."

"Hey, not nice. I'm almost there."

"Uh-huh, I see daylight from this end." As light appeared beside Birdy, Tacy tried to soothe the dog's nerves. "It's okay, sweetie. We just want to help."

Birdy nudged and licked her babies nervously as Brent's hand appeared. She continued to speak to Birdy as he scooped dirt from the area, tunneling out enough so that he could reach for the pups. "Brent, I think you'd better start talking to Birdy before you stick your hand any closer," she warned. "Being a protective mama, she might decide to take a bite out of you."

His low chuckle rumbled softly through the musky darkness. "Boy, you'd love that, wouldn't you?"

She couldn't help smiling. "There have been moments," she tossed back, "very well-deserved moments."

Instead of a comeback, she saw the top of his head come into view behind Birdy. He began talking soothingly to her and the pups. From Tacy's position, she saw Birdy lean back and look at him, her tail thumping wildly. He'd sweet-talked the dog out of all her anxiety that fast. With a sigh, Tacy rose and walked around to find Brent on his belly, his head and one arm hidden beneath the building. It hit her then that he still had on his dress shirt and what looked like new jeans. But that didn't stop him from crawling in the dirt to help her dog.

"Heads up," he called and stuck his hand out of the hole with one squirming, newborn pup.

"Isn't he cute?" Tacy cooed, taking the puppy and cuddling it against her.

"Another one on the way," he called, his voice slightly muffled.

Tacy stroked the puppy's head and gently placed it in the box Brent had brought. He'd thought of everything, and she couldn't help being impressed. The man got under her skin no matter how hard she tried not to let him.

"Six puppies," Brent said, dusting his shirt off and watching Tacy gaze at the squirming pups.

"They are beautiful," she said, petting Birdy's head as she shoved her nose into the box and tried to tend to her babies. "Thanks for helping."

He shrugged and gave her what he hoped was a casual smile. "Anytime. Let's get them home." He held out a hand to Tacy. For a minute he didn't think she'd take it, but she did. And as his hand wrapped around hers, he knew he was going to have a hard time letting it go. And a harder time not pulling her into a hug.

She popped to her feet like a jack-in-the-box and tugged her hand free almost instantly.

He studied her, fighting the need to tease her. He was pushing his luck with her today but he was determined to spend time with her. Determined to share more with her than arguments over riding a horse. "I'll carry the box," he said when she reached for it. "If that's okay with you," he added, just in case she thought he was being bossy.

She just smiled and picked up the shovel. "I'll get this. I know what you're doing, you know."

He grabbed the box and stilled his heart, ready for her to tell him he was barking up the wrong tree if he thought he could get her to fall for him…that it was a bad idea and he knew it. "You do, do you?" he asked.

"Yup. You're trying to steal my dog's affections with all this hero-to-the-rescue stuff." She tossed a fake glare over her shoulder, sashaying away, shovel swinging.

He grinned, watching her, then picked up the box of pups and followed her.

"You know, we get along pretty well when we're not fighting over horses," he said as they left the woods behind and started toward the barn.

"Oh, but that is such an important point. Just think how well we'd get along if you weren't so pigheaded."

Their kiss sprang instantly to mind. "So are

you telling me a horse ride might, um—" he cleared his throat "—make you like me a little more?"

They entered the barn on the back side as they were walking through toward the yard and her truck. She stopped in the center of the alley. "Is that bribery?"

He came to a dead halt and felt his neck heat up. "N-no. That wasn't what I meant." *Sure sounded like it.* "I—" he cleared his throat, since it had suddenly turned about as dry as sawdust "—I only wondered if you would like me more if we didn't have that difference of opinion."

"Probably not," she quipped and strode out of the barn.

What? He followed her to her truck. "You *would* like me," he pushed, unable to stop seeking the truth. "In fact, you do like me, don't you, Tacy Jones?"

Tacy gave him a look that said, "That's what *you* think." Then she took the box of puppies and set them on the front seat of her truck. Birdy jumped onto the floorboard, as if she hadn't just given birth, placed her front paws in the seat and began taking care of her babies. It was easy to see that she would be a great little mother. Unable to stop himself, Brent stepped close to Tacy before she could hop in the driver's seat and leave. "You do, you know," he said. He was near enough to catch the flash of hesitation.

She placed a hand on his chest and held him back.

"Have you called your mom yet and told her you are coming home for Thanksgiving?"

"No. Are you trying to change the subject?"

"Nope. But I have this problem. I'm just not into fear. I'm not into giving in to it. I fight it all the way. You, on the other hand, let it run your life."

"What?"

She tapped her fingers against his chest. "I've figured you out. You were almost the world champion, so you messed your life up. Then, when your bad choices caused you to let your inexperienced sister make a very bad choice, you decided to hide behind that…and you've been doing it ever since. So the answer is no. Even if I do like you, there could never, ever be anything between you and me. Because you look at me and don't see what I'm capable of. You see some en-

tertaining little gal with a feisty side—
someone you're drawn to—but that's it."

He stepped back. "That's not true."

"Yes, it is. I'm a free spirit, Brent, with a
mind and a will of my own. You're drawn to
that, but you'd still try to put me in a cage and
clip my wings. Why, I ask you, would I let
myself fall for someone who'd do that to me?
Simple answer—I wouldn't."

"I didn't sabotage my career on purpose,"
he ground out in a very controlled voice.
"And *I* think you need someone to help keep
you out of trouble."

Her eyes widened. "Maybe I'm wrong as
far as your career is concerned. But I'm not
wrong about how you would treat me. You
just proved it with that statement. If every
man feels that way, I might stay single
forever. God didn't create me to be afraid,
and I won't let someone try to change that."

"I'm not trying to—"

"Look, I'll admit we have great—chemistry—but that's not good enough. I have to go.
Thanks for your help. I'm supposed to work
on the pumpkin chunker today." She nodded
toward the corral. "And *you've* got a bunch
of colts to ride all by your lonesome."

She pulled the door closed, and Brent yanked his hat off and slapped it against his thigh as he watched her leave. He wasn't that person she believed he was…*was* he?

He stomped toward the corral. He was supposed to help with App and Stanley's pumpkin contraption, but he didn't have time. She might be completely wrong about him, but she was right about the colts. They had to be ridden, and he was the only one to do it.

"Tacy, where is your head?" Norma Sue asked. "You've been distracted the whole time you've been here. What's wrong?"

"Nothing," Tacy said. The last thing she was going to do was tell the three ladies known as the matchmaking posse of Mule Hollow that, no matter how brave her words to him were, she was struggling with her feelings for Brent.

Esther Mae dropped the paintbrush into the tray of orange paint. "You're having man troubles, aren't you?"

"Esther Mae," Adela warned softly, "don't push."

"I'm not," Esther Mae said, "but I'm bored and I can't help wanting to help."

Tacy's eyes narrowed. "Ladies, I'm in no need of your services as far as a man is concerned."

Norma Sue set down her screwdriver, her plump face glowing. "That's what everyone says, but what they really mean is, 'Help me.'"

Tacy crossed her arms and frowned sternly at them. "Look, Brent and I are too different. The man is—well, he's handsome, and yes, it's true that I love arguing with him. He's entertaining. But he's also messed up." *What am I doing?* She was asking the question of herself just as three sets of eyes locked on her with expectant anticipation.

"Go on," Norma Sue demanded. "You wouldn't be the first person to notice that men and women are different. That's what makes everything work."

Tacy couldn't believe she was doing this. But looking at them and knowing they had all this experience—it was as if she had to let out her frustrations. Maybe they could help, and suddenly she knew she wanted help. "It would never work. I want to break horses, and he's afraid I'll break my neck— but it's my neck to break! The one thing I'm not going to do is stop because I'm afraid.

That, ladies, is the thing that will keep us apart no matter how attracted to each other we might be." She was breathing hard when she finished.

"Did y'all hear that?" Esther Mae exclaimed, clapping her hands together. "She said they were attracted to each other."

"We heard, all right," Norma Sue said, crossing her arms and scratching her chin.

Tacy knew she'd just made a huge mistake. "Didn't y'all hear the other stuff I said?" she asked.

Dainty Adela smiled kindly, her blue eyes as gentle as the hand she placed on Tacy's arm. "Certainly we did, dear. We heard everything you said. But the question is, did you?"

Huh? "He's controlling."

"He's concerned," Norma Sue said. "Why, my Roy Don used ta try and keep me from working cattle when we first started dating. But when I showed him I could do it as good or better than most men—including him—he gave up. It's not something I have to do every day—especially the rougher stuff now that I'm getting a little older. But when I get the hankerin' to help with a roundup, I do it."

"Well, Brent won't let me near a colt, so

we'll never know if there could have been more between us than this irritating attraction—which may simply come from each of us trying to prove the other wrong."

"Oh, I'm sure that's part of it," Esther Mae said with a sly smile and a bob of her chili-pepper head. "But even then, if you didn't like him, you wouldn't get very far before you got bored or the attraction died."

Tacy cringed. "He'd smother me. I could never stand for that."

"Understandable, dear. But surely if he loves you, he will compromise. If he doesn't, you should walk away and never look back," Adela said. "But my thought on the subject is that God made the heart to know its own mind. Love makes all things possible—even compromise."

"I never said I loved him." Tacy couldn't believe this. She'd heard this town was marriage-crazy, but this was ridiculous.

Norma Sue chuckled. "Maybe not. But there is certainly potential there if you two could get past this horse-breaking thing."

"That horse-breaking thing happens to be my lifelong dream." Frustration tightened its hold on her. It was bad enough that she was—fine—*falling in love,* without having the matchmaking posse of Mule Hollow practically reading her thoughts.

Chapter Fourteen

Brent got tossed on his rear by colt number three. As he pushed himself up out of the dust, he knew it wasn't the colt's fault, but his own. If he'd been concentrating on what he was doing, he'd have deflected the reaction of the threatened animal. Much of horse breaking was concentration, reading the horse before it acted. Same with riding broncs. Concentration, instinct and technique. Today he had none.

Tacy was right. He needed help, and she was available and willing. He just couldn't do it, though. God had forgiven him for his stupidity, but he couldn't make the same mistake again. She was a good rider though, and once he had the saddle on them and a few days in the saddle she should be safe. Right? The two he'd already broke were in need of more time than he was giving them. Plus, Pace was depending on him. Argument done, Brent left the horse standing in the center of the pen and headed for Tacy's place. It was time to compromise a little....

Even if he wasn't comfortable with it, maybe Tacy was right about him being too afraid. Dusting himself off, he climbed out of his truck and strode onto her porch.

He found Birdy and her babies on the porch snuggled together. The proud mama looked up at him and gave him her signature grin. "Hey there, beautiful. How's it going?" he asked, bending down and scratching her between the ears. "You have got some beautiful babies."

The front door opened, and he looked over his shoulder to find Tacy lounging against the door frame, arms and ankles crossed as she watched him. "She looks good," he said. *And so do you.*

"She's very happy. I was actually afraid she was going to start carting them one by one back to the shed or to your barn or something. But thankfully now that the delivery is done, she's decided to stay put."

"And why not? Her favorite person is here watching over her." He smiled at Tacy, but she only gave him a slight lift of one side of her mouth.

"You have dirt on your back," she said. "Interesting, since you weren't digging puppies out from beneath a shed today. Did *you* get tossed, Brent?"

He sighed heavily and stood up, no use denying it. "Yep. I did."

Her chin jutted to the side. "Imagine that. The great Brent Stockwell bit the dust."

He shot her a weary look. "I wasn't concentrating."

"Ohhh, and why was that? Too much to do?"

Because of you. "Yes, you're right. I realized I do need some help."

"So you've come here to ask me to recommend some cowboy to help you ride?"

"Actually, I came to ask you if you'd like to help me ride."

"But not break them."

"This is all I can offer. I won't put you on a green colt. I won't be responsible for hurting you."

Her lips flattened and she studied him hard. He knew she was weighing her options, calculating her chances of changing his mind. She was a smart woman, and she'd realize that he hadn't said the words out loud, but he was offering her the opportunity to watch him break the colts while she rode them. That was more than he wanted to offer her, but it couldn't be helped. When she gave him that sassy smile, he had to admit, even with the trepidation he felt, that he enjoyed very much being responsible for putting that gorgeous grin on her face.

"Okay, I'll do it," she said, the smile spreading like a slow sunrise.

He swallowed and took a deep breath, feeling a catch in his chest just looking at her. "Good," he managed, backing to the edge of the porch. "I—I'll see you tomorrow at sunup. Don't be late." He spun on his heel and headed toward the truck.

"Sunup," she called. "I'll be there with bells on."

He chuckled, got in his truck and tipped his hat to her before backing out of the drive. Tomorrow. It was the beginning of a new headache for him, but he was looking forward to it like nothing he could remember.

* * *

The sun was just a thin sliver of orange on the horizon when Tacy hopped out of her truck. The colts were nothing but dark shapes behind the corral, and for a minute she thought she'd actually beaten Brent out of bed. Then he came strolling casually out of the barn with a saddle on his shoulder. Her heart gave a kick and she kicked it right back down, focusing on why she was here. She was still reeling from his offer and determined to be the best helper he'd ever seen. She understood how hard it was for him to ask her to do this, and she was actually proud of him for doing it. Not that she'd let him know that.

"Is that for me?" she asked as non-chalantly as possible.

"Nope, I'll be using this one. Yours is waiting in the barn."

She almost laughed at that. "Phew, that's a relief. I thought for a minute there you'd gone soft." She strode past him, but his husky chuckle followed her into the barn.

And boy, did she like the sound of it.

She scratched Rabbit between the eyes, then grabbed her saddle and headed to work. Her spirits were soaring as she walked out of the barn. She knew what he'd offered, even though he hadn't said it. He was giving her permission to watch him and learn. He might not be able to put her on an unbroken horse, but he wasn't going to stop her from learning by observation. It wasn't enough, but it was good enough for now. One step at a time. For both of them.

"Who do you want me to start with, boss?"

He opened the holding pen where the three horses he'd saddle-broken were waiting. He shook his head at her comment and held the gate as she squeezed past him. "We'll move down the line from the first broke to the newest."

She set her saddle on the ground and walked easily to the black he'd ridden first. The two-year-olds were still a touch skittish, but the black held its ground for the most part as she spoke softly to him. "We're going to be fast friends, you and me. And you two also," she added, giving the other horses a smile. As if taking her words to heart, the black let her run her hand down his neck. She took her time petting him, letting him get used to her. She could feel Brent watching and wondered what he might be thinking.

She was determined to impress him with her ability. She didn't know why it was so important to her, but she had to make him realize that what happened to his sister wouldn't happen to her. If she could take away the guilt she knew he felt, she would do away with that, too, but that was out of her hands. There were some things that only God could help with.... She looked up at him as he moved to stand beside her. Looking into his solemn eyes, she knew she cared deeply about what was going on behind those eyes and in his heart.

"I think he'll let me on him. What do you think?" she asked, suddenly feeling crowded.

"You're handling yourself well. He's ready. I've had more saddle time with him than the others. But I still want you to be cautious. Is that understood?"

He'd actually praised her. Wow! "I hear you loud and clear, boss." She gave him a teasing smile and headed for her saddle. The sun was now aglow and the sounds of early morning filled the air. Somewhere in the distance, a rooster crowed. Closer, in the woods, the soft twitter of birds drifted on the air and mingled with the snorts of the colts.

"I love this time of morning," she said, carrying the saddle back to the black. Brent had a halter on him now. She hadn't even noticed that he was holding it in his hand. That's how distracted she'd been looking in his eyes and standing near him. She focused again on the horse.

"I'll put that on him," he offered.

"Oh, no, you don't, buster. You hired me to do this, and I'm going to do it. I know how to saddle a horse."

"For the hired help, you sure are bossy," he said, stepping back and letting her do her job.

"Just making sure the boss man gets his money's worth."

He chuckled. "I don't recall there being a paycheck for this job."

She laughed. "Well, that's true. It's the barter system. I know the value of the experience I'm getting out of this deal, and I don't want to shortchange you."

"You won't. I'm sure that you give everything you do your all."

His eyes were serious and knowing he meant the words touched Tacy. She gave him a tight smile and turned back to the black. To her relief, the horse didn't give her any trouble…but then she hadn't expected it to. After all, Brent had been working with him.

She was good. Better than good. She knew what she was doing. Brent saddled up the chestnut, wanting to get a few more rides on it himself before he handed the ornery colt over to Tacy. While he rode around the round pen he was able to observe Tacy and he respected what he saw. He almost felt bad for holding out for so long—almost.

At ten, when she left to get ready for work at the diner, he hated to see her go—not that he let her know it.

"You should come to town for lunch," she said while they were taking saddles off the colts.

"I might do that."

She smiled. "It's good for you to come to town. Everyone enjoys your company, and you know what they say about all work and no play making Brent a dull boy."

He laughed. "So you're telling me I'm dull?"

"No. It was a joke. I find you very intriguing."

His blood warmed at her words. "Is *intriguing* a good thing?"

"It's a very good thing. Me, I'm easily bored, and I have to tell you that you have never bored me, Mr. Stockwell. See you at lunch," she said. "I hate to ride and run, but I've got to get a move on or Sam will not be a happy camper."

"You go. I'll finish up here."

She waved, then jogged to her truck and was off in a flash. Brent didn't move for a long moment, then finally he pulled a brush from the bucket at his feet and began brushing the black colt down. "She's the intriguing one," he said to the colt as he worked. "No question about it."

He was still thinking about Tacy a few minutes later when he walked into the cabin. He wanted to wash his face and hands before heading to the diner. A working cowboy couldn't do much about eating in dusty clothes, but he could at least wash up a little. That had been a rule his mom taught him, and she'd have scolded him but good if he'd shown up at the lunch table without cleaning up. His heart tugged, thinking about those days growing up, when life had been full of learning about horses and dreaming big dreams. He'd sure messed up.

How had he let himself go so wrong? He headed to the small bathroom and washed his face and hands in hot water, scrubbing hard, then rinsed them and stared critically at his reflection in the mirror. The ring of the phone broke the silence and pulled his thoughts out of the past.

His mom's voice on the other end of the line put him right back in it.

Chapter Fifteen

"So, the big festival is this weekend," Tacy said the following day. She'd ridden two horses that morning, gone in for her shift at the café, then returned to the round pen for some saddle time on the chestnut. Brent was there getting ready to start working with the roan he'd begun breaking in the day before just after lunch. They were standing outside the corral and as much as she'd been wanting the opportunity to work these horses, she was finding that she was in no hurry to walk away from Brent. He didn't seem to be in much of a hurry, either.

"Yep. I'm supposed to go help App and Stanley test their catapult this evening."

"So what are their chances?"

He gave her a sly grin. "Better'n most. Those two fellas are pretty with it when it comes to mechanical things. How about your team?"

"They tested it last weekend. I wasn't there, but they said it went a fair distance. They were satisfied. I'm supposed to go there this afternoon, too." She smiled up at him. "I'll bet you never thought you'd be involved in a pumpkin chunkin contest when you signed on for this project."

His eyes widened. "There's a whole bunch of things I didn't know I was signing on for."

"You mean like a nagging next-door neighbor?"

"That'd be an understatement." He took his felt hat off and ran a hand through his slightly damp hair.

It was a hot day for November, eighty degrees in the sunshine, but she hadn't really noticed until then. She'd been far too focused on Brent.

"Well, this nagging neighbor has to ask you one more time if you've decided to go home for Thanksgiving."

The sparkle left his eye, and she wanted to

kick herself. Why, she asked herself, did she insist on messing up a perfectly, somewhat romantic moment…well, maybe *romantic* was stretching it, but really, her heart had been feeling the thrill of his attention and she'd been enjoying it. So why mess it up? *Because you care for him as a whole person, and you want him to get rid of this guilt hanging over him.* True, she thought with a sigh, but still, did she have to bring it up now?

"Tacy, I'm not going home."

"Has your mother called and asked you again?" This was really none of her business, and she half expected him to tell her so.

"Yesterday, if you really want to know. I told her I couldn't make it. I'll be here until next Thursday working horses. That's my job."

"Well, just so you know, I won't be here. I'm heading home Wednesday and coming back late Thursday night. My mom is expecting me, and I can't let her down." Tacy didn't really care if he liked that or not.

"Fine," he said. "I don't care what you do."

"Oh, really. Hey, if you aren't going home to your folks, you're welcome to come along to meet mine." What was she doing?

He obviously was wondering the same

thing since his expression told her that he couldn't believe she'd just offered such a thing. "Okay, so that was a bust," she said, reaching for the gate latch. "Forget I said anything. Stay here all by your lonesome. I'm sure if you decide you want some turkey and company, there are plenty of folks who'd have you over."

She opened the gate and strode into the corral. She was a blooming idiot sometimes. The two of them in a truck the three hundred miles to her folks' ranch would be a disaster. Then there were her brothers. Oh, that would be just wrong. Then again, the idea of Brent getting the Jones brothers' interrogation treatment would actually make those scare tactics seem funny.

No one would ever know what it had been like growing up as the little sister of the Jones brothers. Boys had been so terrified of her big brothers that dates didn't usually hang around after the first or maybe the second night out.

At least she was living her own life now; it was her choice not to have a social life rather than her big brothers' choice. Jacob, Lucas, Tanner, and the worst of them all,

Zack. Zack took his role as the eldest to the extreme when it came to his baby sister. Of course, it had been a little while since she'd given them any reason to show their protective instincts.

She was an adult now. Surely they were past all that. It didn't matter anyway because there was no way on earth that Brent Stockwell would take her up on her offer.

And that was a good thing. Right?

"Okay, here goes nothin'," App said, breaking into Brent's wandering thoughts. Grinning, App reached out and released the lever.

Instantly, a pumpkin launched skyward like a torpedo in open waters—only instead of flying straight it went slightly to the left and smashed through the window of App's barn!

"Did ya see *that?*" Applegate bellowed. Both he and Stanley were jumping and dancing a jig—hooting and hollering with joy.

Brent gave a short laugh. "Well, I'll be," he said in quiet disbelief, staring at the hole in Applegate's barn. It might have been off target by a bit, but App's barn was about seven hundred feet away. Not bad for a first shot.

After a few minutes of celebrating, App stopped dancing and turned penetrating eyes on Brent. "So what kind of intel have ya got from Tacy?"

"Now, Applegate, I told you she's not telling me anything."

"Nothin'?"

He shook his head. "She's been sworn to secrecy, and from what I can tell her lips are sealed."

Stanley studied him silently. His bushy brows dipped, and he rubbed his chin. "You tried ta sweet-talk her?"

Brent gave a choked laugh. "No, I have not tried to sweet-talk her."

That got him a glare of disbelief from both men. App was the first to react. "What's wrong with ya?"

"Yeah," Stanley added. "You're out thar riding with her fer the last few days and ya ain't made a move *yet?*"

Brent crossed his arms across his chest and cocked his head to the side, meeting their glares with one of his own. "Fellas, I'm not going to sweet-talk Tacy to get intel for the two of you. Just forget it."

"Well, fine and dandy," Stanley said. "But

what about just sweet-talkin' that girl fer the fun of it? What's wrong with you, man?"

"Yeah, that thar is a good little gal. Half this town's cowboy population has been dawdling around like lovesick pups since she come ta town, and yor the first one I seen her be interested in."

"Yeah," Stanley echoed.

That got his attention. "What exactly do you mean?"

"She likes you, cowboy, and we think yor okay. We ain't said nothing about yer past mistakes since you arrived. We figure every man's gonna make mistakes in his life. We've been watchin' ya, and we're proud ta see that you seem like you've put yor wilder side aside."

"Yeah," Stanley said again. "So we figured not ta stand in yor way when we seen how Tacy looks at you. But what we ain't understanding is why you ain't making no move ta woo her. Are you daft, man?"

Brent was at a loss for words. His past was no secret. Some of the men had recognized him, and it was no big deal. But App and Stanley had never said anything. Not that that was the reason he was speechless. It was the other info that had him gaping like a fish out of water. "How exactly does Tacy look at me?"

App's mouth dropped, forming a cascade of wrinkles. "You mean ta tell us you *are* daft?"

Chapter Sixteen

It was dark when Tacy pulled into her driveway. There had been several women out at Norma Sue's to watch the first shot of the unbelievably cool catapult. Lacy was there, along with Sugar Rae Denton and her best friend, the local real estate agent, Haley Bell Sutton—who also happened to be Applegate's granddaughter. Haley Bell told Tacy that she just loved it when Norma Sue riled up her grandpa because he secretly enjoyed it. Tacy thought about that all evening. It was clear that Haley loved her grandpa and wanted good things for him. Tacy wanted good things for Brent, too, the stubborn mule.

She was pulling to a stop when she saw headlights on the deserted dirt road. It was an access road to part of Clint Matlock's ranch, and this house and the cabin Brent lived in were the only two places on it. Sure enough, it was the cowboy, coming home from App's, probably. She closed the truck and was walking toward the porch when he slowed down. His window was open and he stared across at her in the moonlight. Then he turned his truck into her drive and headed slowly her way. Tacy's heart was thundering in her chest as he came to a stop. She'd been around him almost every day for the past three weeks, but this was the first time she'd seen him under the stars, in the moonlight, with the soft mewling of cattle in the distance like a Texas serenade. She suddenly felt nervous about him being here. In this setting, she simply didn't trust herself.

"Evening," he said, pulling up behind her truck. He didn't get out, but let his arm hang out the window as his disarming gaze connected with hers. It was a wonder she could hear him over the racket her heart was making in her chest.

"Evening," she managed. Birdy left her pups behind and came to greet him. He cut his motor and stepped to the ground. Stooping to Birdy's level, he gave her a good ear rub while looking up at Tacy with a grin that didn't help her heart calm down at all.

"Have fun tonight?" he asked.

She nodded. "You?" she managed, her stomach churning now. Until Brent, she hadn't given much thought to how a man's arms would feel holding her close or how his lips would feel against hers. She'd simply focused on her plans and that had been all she needed. Brent had totally disrupted everything. When it came to him, she was so out of her comfort zone she felt like a schoolgirl.

She swallowed when he stood up and tucked his fingers into the pockets of his jeans.

His lips lifted into a slanted smile. "I have to warn you that the competition is going to be tough."

If he only knew what she'd seen tonight, he might not be thinking that. Norma Sue was a pure wizard when it came to mechanical things. Tacy couldn't believe it. Norma Sue's contraption was interactive and required lots of "pedal power." "Let's just say that after what I experienced tonight, I know we are up for the challenge. Saturday promises to be one exciting afternoon."

"Yep," he said, as an oddly awkward silence stretched between them. He was wearing a Western shirt that was so white it almost glowed in the bright moonlight. His shoulder muscles tensed beneath it as Tacy's gaze drifted to his chest. She felt a longing to lay her head on his shoulder and wrap her arms around his neck. There was just something so compelling about Brent that she'd never felt about anyone before. Feeling strange, she was afraid to look him in the eye.

"It's a nice night," he said, his voice hoarse as he ran his boot over a rock. Tacy's gaze dropped to his boot, and she watched him worry the rock back and forth. *Was he nervous, too?*

She took a deep breath and let it out slowly. Then, looking at him, she yanked a thumb over her shoulder toward the porch. "Would you like to sit on the porch and have a drink? I've got soda and tea." What was she doing?

His lips did that slow lift to one side, sending a shiver of happiness over Tacy as he said, "That sounds good."

"Good—I mean, great." She spun on her heel and hurried up the walk, willing herself to get a grip. If this kept up she'd be hyperventilating before long.

When she reached the porch, she suddenly realized that there was only the porch swing to sit on. While she stood there contemplating what to do, Brent strode over and took one side of the swing. He leaned back, placed his arm across the top and smiled. "This is nice. Come on over."

"Um, didn't you want something to drink?"

"I changed my mind. Sit." He watched her closely. He was probably getting a kick out of seeing her so flustered. She couldn't even remember the last time this had happened to her…probably when Carl Prier had tried to hold her hand on the bus back in sixth grade. Carl was the first boy she'd ever liked, but she'd been too shy then to say anything. Then she'd made the mistake of telling her brothers. After that, Carl had made sure to sit as far away from her on the bus as possible. Not exactly what she'd wanted.

So began her "love" life with four protective brothers and a dad who was worse than all of them put together.

Well, not tonight. She strode to the swing and sank down beside Brent—making sure to leave a space between them. Not looking at him, she stared at the sky. From the swing she had a straight shot at the huge moon. It was beautiful—and romantic.

"It's a nice night," she said, and mentally slapped herself. They'd already established that.

"Yep," he said, pushing the swing with his toe and causing her to lean back.

"Are you going to ride in the rodeo at Clint's Saturday night?" It had been something she was going to ask him, but it had kept slipping her mind.

"I haven't decided."

She could feel his arm behind her neck and tried to concentrate. "You should. It would be easy pickings for you."

He chuckled at that. "Maybe not. There are cowboys around here who've worked with horses and cattle all their lives. They may not have competed in the professional rodeo world, but that's probably because they were too busy actually working to haul across the nation after a championship buckle."

Tacy stared at him. He meant what he said, and she liked that about him, too. He didn't boast about his accomplishments, but rather downplayed them. She knew he hadn't said that about the cowboys just to be saying it. He believed it was true. And what did she know? It might be true. Not every cowboy could afford to devote his time to seeking out points almost every weekend during the season in order to rack up enough to put him in contention for Vegas.

Tacy cleared her throat and smiled, relaxing her back against the swing and suddenly enjoying the feel of his arm practically draped across her shoulders.

"Are you enjoying working with the horses?" he asked after a few moments of silence.

"You know I am."

"Good. I really appreciate your helping me. Especially after the way I've treated you."

"Okay, who are you and what have you done with the real Brent Stockwell?" she asked, smiling and suddenly feeling more like herself.

He laughed. "I thought that would throw you."

"Well, it did. I know what happened. When you were at Applegate's, you got hit on the head with a pumpkin when it was shot out of the catapult."

"Hey, telling you I know I've been rough on you isn't that big a deal."

"Yes, it is," she said, smiling warmly. Pulling her feet up onto the swing, she wrapped her arms around her knees as he continued to rock them gently.

Right now she was just going to enjoy herself.

"So you're going home next Wednesday night?" he asked, tugging her ponytail gently. The action was unexpected and touched her heart.

Turning her head, she rested her chin on her elbow. "Mmm-hmm," she murmured, then pulled her head out of the fog and came back to reality. "It should be interesting. All my brothers will be there, so it will be loud and I'll be picked on mercilessly."

"That bad, huh?"

She laughed. "I'm little sis and they are my sworn protectors. I think when I was born Dad made them swear an oath or something that they'd take care of me for life."

"I can't see you letting them push you around."

"There are *four* of them and only one of me. They are big and brawny, Texas-born-

and-bred, protective and pushy, but I wasn't a complete pushover—you tried pushing me around." She chuckled when his brows dipped at that. "You remind me of them. It sounds as if you were pretty protective of your sister, too." The minute she said the words she knew she'd made a mistake. His eyes grew troubled, and he looked out toward the moon. Birdy came and rested her chin on his knee as he stopped rocking the swing. He gently rubbed her head, lost in thought. She'd known something was different when he'd gotten out of the truck. She really felt it now.

"You know you miss her," Tacy pushed, gently.

"I do. I'm proud of her, too. She's handled her troubles like a real trouper."

"Then why not go see her? I'm sure she's longing to see you."

"Tacy, don't go there. You don't understand."

She turned in the seat to face him. Folding one leg beneath her, she laid an arm on top of his on the back of the seat. "Try me."

He studied her with one of those long stares of his, and she knew he was weighing his options. She found herself praying that he would trust her with what bothered him so.

She wasn't sure if anyone else saw in his eyes how much his past haunted him…but she saw it and that haunted her, too. She wanted Brent to find peace. Was that her real purpose here?

Brent took a deep breath of the sultry night air and felt like he needed to shake himself out of the mood he was in. First Jess, then Applegate and Stanley told him they thought Tacy was crazy about him. He'd been lying when he'd tried to ignore what he was feeling toward her. He'd been trying to figure her out, but the woman was tough to read. In some ways, she had as many walls built up as he did.

Looking at her now, he knew he wanted to level with her. "Tacy, I let everyone in my life down," he said, "including myself. That's not an easy thing to fix."

"But it can be done. And you don't strike me as a quitter."

He lifted a brow. "This isn't a competition we're talking about."

"Well, no. It's much more important than that."

Her words hit him straight on. "True. Still, when a man loses his self-respect, he doesn't get it back easily. I've hurt everyone in my family. My dad, my mom and my little sister. She's fine now, getting stronger every day, but like I told you before, it's only by the grace of God."

"Maybe you need to let yourself have some of that grace. You know, God doesn't just pass it out to some people. It's there for everyone."

"I know God's forgiven me. I know He has the grace to help me through this, but this isn't about God. This is about me." Brent didn't know if he could make her or anyone else understand what was in his heart or his head. He held Tacy's questioning gaze and found himself wanting her to understand. "I thought I'd grow up to be a man of integrity. I never thought that I'd be the jerk who let his talent and good fortune blow up his ego. That bothers me. I lost faith in myself."

He thought she'd say something, but instead she ran her hand gently over his arm as if urging him to keep going. As if letting him know it was okay. The gentle act reached inside the dark corners of his heart.

Suddenly, he needed to continue. "The weirdest part was that I'd never been a partier before. I'd been a hard worker, dedicated to making my dream of a world championship a reality. My family was proud of me. But somehow, when it counted the most, I let it all go to my head. I thought I *deserved* all the attention I started getting."

"You're not the first person that's happened to, and I'm sure you won't be the last."

He blinked hard, startled by her words. "So I suppose that fixes everything," he ground out, feeling instantly about as grizzly as it got.

"*No,* I didn't say that. I was merely trying to help you see that you aren't the first guy to mess up," she said. "Brent, you told me early on that the man in those tabloids was dead. Do you believe that?"

"Yes, I do. That wasn't really me. I don't date reality TV stars in real life. That was me in my fool's world. Even though most of the stuff they wrote wasn't even true, I was still out of control. I didn't realize how much until I went home and…" His voice trailed off and he stared at his boots. He'd stopped pushing the swing again. "So there, now you know pretty much every dirty secret there is to know. If you were smart, you'd get up, go inside and forget all about me."

She was looking at him with calm, kind eyes. He couldn't read what she was thinking, but he waited as she processed his words. Finally, she smiled and her eyes lit up as they touched his lips. That one look sent his pulse into a gallop. He leaned toward her and dipped his head. Tacy started to close her eyes, then shoved him in the shoulder.

"Forget it, buster," she said hoarsely, breaking the romantic spell. "You're not getting me to give up on the horse breaking that easy. As I said before, you're not drunk and I'm not your sister. I think you underestimate both of us."

Chapter Seventeen

"Isn't this is a great crowd?" Lacy exclaimed as Tacy found her at the sign-up booth for the "Punkin Chunkin" event.

"I thought I wasn't going to find a parking space," Tacy agreed, scanning the crowd for people of interest…number one on the list—okay, the only one on the list—Brent Stockwell. They'd both been up since five trying to get some riding in on the horses before reporting to the event at ten. Brent had offered her a ride into town, but she'd made up an excuse to drive herself. Ever since the night before last, when she'd sat beside him on the porch swing, she'd been struggling to keep her distance from the man. True, she was working with him, but she'd forced that into perspective and kept all conversation in her usual flippant tone. They remained at a standstill over her desire to break horses— and to see him head home to his family for Thanksgiving.

"How's everything going?" Lacy asked, plopping a flamingo-pink-nailed hand on her hip. There was no question about what everything she was asking about.

"We're like two hardheaded mules playing tug-of-war!"

Lacy's electric blue eyes sparkled. "Isn't that fun? I still love to give Clint a hard time. I keep that man on his toes. You're good for Brent."

Lacy surprised Tacy by reaching out and hugging her. "You know God sends people into our lives when we need them—did I already tell you that? Anyway, I believe He's at work here. If there is anything I can do, you just give me a holler. And remember, I'm praying for good things to happen."

Tacy laughed, feeling uneasy. She knew what *good things* Lacy was insinuating, but the big question was what *good things* did Tacy want to happen?

"Thanks," she said and meant it. "Well, I

see Norma Sue and the ladies so I'd better get my pedal power over there before they have a conniption."

Lacy laughed. "Are you up for the challenge?"

"I think so. But honestly, Brent said App and Stanley's pumpkin test went really well, so I don't know what to expect. How many other teams are here?"

"Just five. For our first contest and only local advertising, that's a nice turnout. It'll be fun."

"Hope so." Tacy waved, then jogged toward her team. It was hard to miss them, since Esther Mae had on a hot-pink jogging suit with a purple-and-pink scarf tied in her red hair. She stood out in the crowd like a beacon. Plus, the bright orange catapult they'd built was pretty big and dazzling itself.

Halfway across the field, she spotted Brent. He was leaning against a contraption twenty feet away from her team, watching her jog toward him. As she went past, he tipped his hat and smiled, and she almost tripped over her own two feet.

Yup, no doubt about it. Today was going to be very interesting.

* * *

"It's gonna work," Applegate grumbled from his kneeling place behind Brent.

"I tell you, it ain't," Stanley countered. "Last night, it barely shot them pumpkins two hundred feet!"

"I made some adjustments since then."

"And what do you call what yor doin' right now? The competition is almost ready ta start and you got yer wrenches out and yer hands greasy. That don't put much confidence in a man, ya know."

Brent had zoned out the minute Tacy came into view jogging across the pasture.

Who was he kidding? She jogged by, and he planted his boots so that he didn't follow—not that it was that far. He had to admit he was glad to see that their teams were side by side. It promised to be a very entertaining afternoon in more ways than one. Who wouldn't want to spend the afternoon listening to App and Stanley grumble at each other? He wondered if older women gave each other as hard a time as older men. It didn't look like it from here. The ladies' camp was not far away, and Esther Mae and Norma Sue looked like they were getting along just fine. They were checking out what looked to be a bicycle attached to their catapult. It appeared that pedaling would tighten the tension and release their catapult. Maybe that was why they weren't grumbling. They didn't have to worry about their motor failing.

He had to admit, though, that if the motorized version behaved as it was supposed to, the pedal-powered counterpart would be at a huge disadvantage.

And, grumpy as they were, he knew App and Stanley were already patting themselves on the back.

Still, he wouldn't count the ladies out just yet. Tacy was on that team and probably the power source. He crossed his arms and watched her give first Norma Sue and then Esther Mae each a hug. Instantly, he thought about defecting to their team if he'd get a hug for it.

He had it bad and he knew it. The green-eyed gal had worked her way into his every thought—and into his heart. She was stubborn and aggravating. But he knew there was something between them that defied logic. She felt it, too, and he thought she was fighting the attraction just as hard as he was.

With good reason.

They were not right for each other.

They would butt heads over and over and over again. She wanted the one thing he would never give her…could never give her. She wouldn't be happy without it, and that would mean he wouldn't be happy. It would never work. Knowing that should make it easy for him to put her out of his mind. But it was far more complicated than that.

He'd never felt this—this pull toward anyone. He liked the way she looked, the way she spoke, the way she carried herself— walking, riding, jogging. You name it, he just liked looking at her. It went even deeper than that, though. He liked her humor and her laugh, the sassy way she came back at him with her quick wit. He liked listening to her talk about finding her own way in life. He admired her for pushing herself to fulfill her dream, even though her overprotective family tried to hold her back. And he liked how she still cared for her family. Tacy Jones had a great heart. She knew exactly who she was and, as far as he could tell, she'd never wavered from being that person. She was who she was. Maybe that came from her strong-but-understated faith. And maybe that faith, that compass she had that grounded her, was what he admired most about her. Maybe that was why she had no fear—maybe that was why she refused to live with fear. Her words rang in his head: *As I said before, you're not drunk and I'm not your sister. I think you underestimate both of us.*

All night, he'd thought about those words—and thought about her. He hadn't expected her to hold fast to her plan after he'd shared his concern so openly and completely. No, she wasn't his sister. He hadn't been drunk or even taken a drink since that day in the arena. But underestimate himself? She thought he was underestimating himself when, in fact, he'd already lowered the bar so low there was no estimating to it anymore. As for her, he knew she could do whatever she set her mind to, including breaking horses. He just couldn't be the one to teach her.

Suddenly, feeling grumpier than App and Stanley put together and needing a distraction, Brent pushed away from the catapult just as Lacy stepped up to the microphone. The festivities were about to begin.

* * *

"Load 'er in there, Brent," Applegate commanded loudly, standing straight and tall as a general.

Brent carefully set the pumpkin into the pocket—having been told by Applegate that placement affected trajectory. He certainly didn't want to be blamed for the projectile going astray. This was *serious* business. "How's that look?" he asked.

"Looks good ta me," Stanley yelled over the hum of the motor.

"Maybe tilt it to the right a touch," App countered.

Norma Sue was standing beside Stanley, and she looped a thumb around one of her overall straps and frowned. "That thing is straight, Applegate, and you know it. Straight or not doesn't matter, though."

"That's right. Nothing's going to beat us," Esther Mae gushed, leaning around Norma Sue. The pink-and-purple scarf tied like a headband in her red hair distracted Brent momentarily. The two women were like night and day. Norma Sue was a robust woman fond of ranch work and overalls. Esther Mae had on a bright pink jogging suit—one of those shiny outfits that made swishing noises when she walked. He knew it did because she'd been swishing from one catapult to the other for the last hour as everyone waited for the competition to get under way.

Farther behind them he saw Tacy biting her lip to keep from smiling. He caught and held her gaze and enjoyed the twinkle in her eyes as he lifted a teasing brow at her. She flashed one back at him and he savored the moment.

App grunted loudly. "You gonna jest stand thar ogling Tacy or ya gonna step back so I kin fire this thang?"

Brent laughed. "I'm stepping back now, sir. Fire away."

"You know, you could just give up now, App," Norma Sue yelled. "No harm in admitting defeat."

Applegate gave her a glare and triggered the punkin chunker. There was a loud "thwunk" as the tension released the bands and the pumpkin launched into the air. All heads turned and watched as the pumpkin sailed left two hundred feet and landed in the concession stand.

App and Stanley stood in stunned silence. Esther Mae and Norma Sue hooted with laughter, as did the crowd behind them. Brent wasn't exactly sure how he felt. It was funny, no doubt about it, but it also was not right. He knew App's pumpkin chunker could do better.

Tacy winked at him when he glanced her way, and he couldn't help grinning at the mischievous glimmer in her eyes.

Of course, when App and Stanley turned toward him, their gazes weren't nearly so pleasant. "Hey," Brent said. "That wasn't my fault. But if you give me just a second, I think I can fix it."

"How you gonna fix that?" Stanley asked, clearly mortified by such a poor showing.

"If you kin fix it," App snapped, "then have at it."

Norma Sue grinned broadly and slapped App on the back. "Go ahead and concede, ya ole goat!"

"No," Brent interjected. "App's machine is going to give you ladies a run for your money, mark my word."

"I'll believe it when I see it," Esther Mae said.

"Don't be bad, Esther Mae," said Adela, standing quietly off to the side. "It's not nice to gloat."

Brent walked over to the catapult and quickly adjusted the bands. He'd realized that it wasn't his pumpkin placement but a slight difference in the balance of the bands between levers that had accounted for the dismal showing.

Within moments, the men had the next pumpkin in the slot, and away it flew, just like a clay pigeon out *across* the field—just the way it was supposed to go.

It looked so good flying out into the wild blue yonder that several cowboys whistled, and Applegate's chest puffed out with pride as the pumpkin arched and finally began its downward descent.

"What do ya thank about them thar apples?" App asked Norma Sue and Esther Mae.

Norma had both hands on her hips and was squinting at the pumpkin as it crashed onto the field. "I think you'd better hold on to your hat, App. C'mon, gals. Let's show these boys how it's really done!"

"So how does it feel to be a winner?"

Tacy jumped at the sound of Brent's voice so close to her ear. "Great," she said, looking over her shoulder at him. His eyes were crinkled at the edges. "I hope the old codgers team is doing all right."

Brent laughed. "You saw how App acted. He took his defeat in stride, but I hate to see what kind of contraption he and Stanley will bring to the festivities next year."

Tacy chuckled, knowing it was true. "Norma Sue and Esther will hold this over them until they're beaten."

"Will you let your boss buy you a glass of Adela's famous lemonade?"

Tacy turned to face him and nodded. "Sure." It was a gorgeous day. "I have to say I'm glad the punkin chunkin contest is over."

"You and me both. I enjoyed it, though."

They were walking through the small crowd toward the food booths. From what Tacy had been told, this was a smaller festival than most they held. "I like this town," she said. "It's like a warm piece of apple pie."

"What does that mean?" Brent laughed.

He placed his hand at her back as they went single file through a clump of people. Tacy liked the feel of his hand—it was as if they were a couple. Focus, Tacy, focus. "It," she started, and had to remember what she'd said—apple pie. "You know, apple pie is home and hearth. Grandma and Grandpa. Good friends and family. That's what I meant. Mule Hollow is that. Even when they're grumpy at each other."

"Only you would put it that way. But you're right."

They got in line at the lemonade stand and Tacy faced him—missing the feel of his hand when he crossed his arms and tucked his fingers into the crooks. He was looking at her with a strange glint in his eyes, and for a moment she fantasized that he'd tucked his hands tightly into place in order to keep from tucking them around her.... Right.

Brent paid for two glasses of lemonade, and they started walking toward the open field where the crowd thinned. "So," she said, taking a deep breath, "have you thought any more about what I said?" She knew she didn't have to elaborate.

"Tacy, it's not that I'm underestimating you. I know you think that, but that isn't it. I like that you have no fear—"

"Whoa, I didn't say I don't have fear," she clarified as she stopped walking to look up at him. "I have fear." *Like right now, looking at you.* She felt like she was speeding down a dirt road with the lights off. It was exhilarating and scary at the same time. "I said I don't let fear rule my life. I refuse to let it dictate my actions or choices."

His eyes darkened with intensity just before he pulled them away from her and studied the stand of trees a hundred yards away. "You're a strong woman, Tacy."

"Because I make myself be."

"You don't get it. I'm not a softy. I'm no deadbeat, afraid of my own shadow. It's just that I take care of what I care about—of who I care about. That's the way my dad brought me up. That's the reason he and I don't get on. I let my focus get distracted and went crazy for a year and it cost me. It cost Tina more. I care what happens to you, Tacy, and that's why I can't be the one to teach you to break horses."

Her heart went to thrumming with his words.

"Just like your dad and your brothers, I want to see you live for decades to come. A ride on an unbroken horse isn't worth what would be lost if you got injured or—"

So they were back at square one. Tacy hung her head and studied her boots. She blinked against the tears that threatened to overwhelm her. Dumb tears. The song "Cowgirls Don't Cry" played in her head and she swallowed hard. She would not do this. *Why did his words hurt her so?* She knew she was falling in love with him—had already fallen in love with him. She hadn't meant for it to happen or wanted it to happen. But it was true. She'd fallen in love with a man she could not have a future with. Sucking in a shaky breath, she lifted her gaze to his and forced her voice to hold steady. "And therein lies the problem. My safety isn't *your* concern. It's mine." She could easily solve the problem, or so it seemed, by simply hiring someone else to teach her, and then maybe she and Brent could… No, that would only be a bandage on a deeper problem. The man she let herself love had to accept her as she was. Brent didn't.

Turning, she walked away, her heart pounding so hard it threatened to burst into a million tiny pieces.

Chapter Eighteen

There was food everywhere. Tacy stood beside the tea pitchers and filled glasses with ice.

"You sure are quiet today," Lacy said as she filled the glasses with the tea. "What happened yesterday?"

"Nothing, why do you ask?"

"Because," Norma Sue said, pausing to pick up a glass of tea, "after we whupped the grumpy old men, every one of us saw you and Brent making goo-goo eyes at each other. Then we saw you run out of the party."

"I was not making goo-goo eyes. We got lemonade together and then I went home."

"In a huff," Esther Mae said as she joined the surprise inquisition.

Tacy got distracted by Esther Mae's orange

hat, complete with tiny pumpkin tassels hanging from its brim.

"I was tired," she said. "Remember, I was the one who had to ride the bike."

"You weren't even winded," Norma Sue said. "Don't give me that. You two looked like y'all were having a good time and then, boom, you were out of there."

"Looked suspicious to me," Lacy said, grinning like a lunatic.

Tacy glared at her and got a teasing wink in return.

"C'mon, c'mon, spill," Lacy needled. "You can't leave the girlfriends hanging here. Y'all had a sweetheart spat. That's why Brent is conspicuously missing from the festivities."

"I don't know why he isn't here. The man is antisocial."

"As I remember last week, you ran out early and he did, too—"

"Not as early as he wanted." Esther Mae harrumphed. "Norma dragged the poor boy out on the volleyball court and wouldn't let him get away."

Norma grinned. "I think he finally sneaked out when I was getting a rock out of my boot."

Tacy had never seen a volleyball game quite like a Mule Hollow Church of Faith game. Norma Sue usually wore crop pants with her boots, and many of the cowboys played wearing their starched Sunday jeans, boots and dress shirts. It was a very odd-looking crew, but fun. She hadn't stuck around last week because of Birdy—or at least Birdy had been her excuse.

"The point is," Esther Mae continued, "we sense trouble in paradise." She wagged her head, making her pumpkins dance.

Tacy groaned. "What Brent Stockwell does isn't my concern. We were just getting lemonade."

"The man didn't take his eyes off you the whole time you were riding that bike," Esther Mae said.

Tacy gave her an impatient look. "How would you know? You were watching the pumpkins skyrocket past App and Stanley's."

"I glanced Brent's way," Esther Mae said indignantly, "briefly."

"So fill us in."

"Norma Sue, has anyone ever told you that you're very pushy?"

"Kind of remind you of yourself, don't I?"

Tacy had to laugh. "We cowgirls have to stick together, I guess."

Norma Sue grinned. "You'd better believe it. Now why is it that you and this handsome cowboy are still sidestepping around each other instead of Texas two-stepping together?"

"Why, Norma," Esther Mae gasped, "that was so poetic."

"I don't date, remember?"

"Yep, I know what you said," Lacy said. "I said the same thing. But when Clint came along, I had to change my plans."

Tacy gave up. "Brent won't teach me. He won't let me on an unbroken colt. I've already told y'all I can't live with that."

All three women gaped at her.

"You haven't gotten on one of them colts yet?" Norma Sue asked, ramming her hand on her hip.

Tacy started to toss out a comeback, then stopped. Why hadn't she?

"I told you to make *fireworks,*" Lacy said. "Did you not understand that I meant for you to go over there and get on whatever horse in that corral you wanted to get on? Believe me when I tell you that Sheri and

Pace fully expected you, of all people, to push Brent's buttons."

"Sounds just like our Sheri," Esther Mae agreed.

"All we're saying," Lacy said, "is you aren't acting like yourself. The Tacy who came to town a few weeks ago would have figured out a way to get what she wanted by now. It doesn't make sense that you are suddenly complacent and letting him just tell you no."

"Unless—" Norma Sue beamed "—there's a little thang called love goin' on."

Tacy had to get control of this conversation. "Y'all, I came to the churchwide Thanksgiving dinner to celebrate the occasion with my friends—not to get dragged over the coals."

Adela appeared through the throngs of people at the food tables. She took one look at Tacy and walked over. "That is the face of an ambush victim if ever I saw one. Are they giving you a hard time?" she said with a knowing smile.

"We're trying to help her," Norma Sue and Esther Mae said in unison.

Adela placed a willowy hand on Tacy's arm. "I couldn't help but notice that Brent isn't here. I've been wondering if something was wrong. Does he have a hard time with Thanksgiving?"

Tacy relaxed with Adela. "I think right now he'd have problems at any holiday, but Thanksgiving is especially hard for him."

"You don't say," Norma Sue said as she and everyone else mulled over what Tacy had just revealed.

"I think you are a good friend to him. We'll fix him up a nice big plate of food and you can run it over."

Tacy started to protest, stopped and realized she'd already been thinking about doing that anyway. Even mad at him, she still had a need to make him feel better. She just wished he'd get that feeling toward her sometime.

"Yep, yep! That's a great idea, Adela," Lacy exclaimed. "And while you're there, you can hop on a horse and show that cowboy what you've got. Break the mold he's stuck in." She cocked a brow and grinned at Tacy.

Tacy laughed. "You are incorrigible, as my mom would say."

"She must have called you that a lot," Lacy said.

"Yes, among other things."

"I don't get it," Norma Sue said. "I see you as a mischievous kid and teen determined to do what you wanted to do."

"I was," Tacy admitted.

"But weren't you raised on a horse ranch?" Norma prodded.

"Yes."

"With brothers and a dad who train and break horses?"

Tacy nodded. She didn't like feeling pressed. She saw a light go on in the robust woman's eyes. "Ah, I get it. You don't want to chance falling in love because you have a problem saying no to the men you love."

"No. I came here, didn't I?"

Lacy was watching her very closely. In fact, all the ladies' eyes now drilled into her. "Yes," she admitted, "it's true. I came here because if I stayed back home I knew I wouldn't ever go against what my daddy wanted me not to do."

Esther Mae gasped. "And you ran straight into the same situation. Only instead of loving this man, you've fallen *in* love with him and that's why you've put your light under a bushel!"

Tacy swallowed past the lump in her

throat. There was no way she could deny any of this. Not with these four. They were too observant. And they cared about her. "When you love someone, you give up certain things. That's why I was so determined not to date. I couldn't take the chance of falling in love because I knew how I would react if the man I fell in love with had a problem with me breaking horses. Or even training them. I knew I needed to have my career well under way before I fell in love. That's what you do for someone you love, right? You take their feelings, wants and needs into consideration?"

Lacy's brow crinkled. "To an extent. But, Tacy, you don't just give up everything you've ever wanted or dreamed of."

Tacy dropped her jaw. "Lacy, I see how you look at Clint. Are you telling me you wouldn't give up your salon if he asked? No, the better word is—if he *needed* you to? The same goes for any of you. I know how much each of you love your husbands. You'd do whatever you had to if they needed you to."

They gave in to that with nods and murmured yeses.

"But the same is true for my Hank," Esther

Mae declared, an obstinate expression locked onto her face. "He'd do the same for me. When it comes to things like that, we work it out. I'm kind of stubborn myself, and in my early days I was a little hard to handle—I know that may be hard to believe now."

Norma Sue rolled her eyes. "Hardly," she said.

Tacy had to smile, despite everything. "I can see where you might have been a touch feisty."

Esther Mae beamed. "The thing is, we don't have all the answers."

"And they certainly don't." Adela smiled. "Come on, everyone, it's time to give poor Tacy a rest while we give thanks to the Lord for all the blessings we have here in our little town. I believe Pastor Allen is about to begin."

Lacy leaned in close. "You're off the hook for now, girlfriend—but you can bet we're talking about this later."

Tacy chuckled, despite the stomach churning that was going on inside her. As the pastor called everyone's attention, she focused.

She was here in this lovely town among all these heartwarming—if overly nosy—people, and she was so glad to be here. God really was great. She had been so blessed in her life. Coming here, she'd been set to soar with her dreams. She'd known who she was—where she wanted to go with her life— and she'd had a plan for exactly how she was going to get there. She hadn't expected everything to be totally turned upside down from day one. She certainly hadn't expected to fall for the hardheaded, obstinate man who was at the corrals alone with his colts and his stubborn heart. The pastor asked all those gathered there to bow their heads. In a deep, wise voice he said a beautiful prayer of thanksgiving for all the blessings the people of Mule Hollow had been given. He also thanked the Lord for the gift of eternal life He offers each and every person. As the pastor said his prayer, Tacy said her own. She thanked God for giving her dreams, ability and the grit and determination to see those dreams to fruition…and she thanked him for Brent. It didn't matter in that moment that knowing and loving Brent threatened everything she'd worked for and dreamed of. It didn't matter that she was torn up inside. In that moment she simply prayed for Brent.

Then she prayed for patience, because a

storm was brewing as far as Brent was concerned. The ladies had no idea how bad she had it.

Or how confused she was.

Tacy was different. She'd been different since the festival when she left him standing in the field. He'd let her go, watched her stomp across the field, skirt the festival and climb into her truck and leave. He'd walked back more slowly and done the same thing. He hadn't gone back to Pace's, though. He'd driven around trying to make sense of what was happening between him and Tacy. He knew there was no denying that he'd fallen for her. Little good it did him.

He hadn't come to Mule Hollow to fall in love. This wasn't the time in his life when he needed that—he didn't feel worthy of the love of a good woman. He knew that Tacy was changing that.

Something about the way she pushed and prodded him, teased and challenged him, made him know that he would never lose sight of the man he was meant to be. That didn't alter the clear fact that he wasn't the right man for Tacy.

And that simply killed him.

She was so upset with him that she'd put her walls back up. That was the difference in her behavior, and he knew it. He'd crossed the line into a realm of Tacy's world that no other cowboy had been able to do. Jess had been right about that. But Brent didn't know exactly how right the cowboy had been until now, until he was sent back to the position of every other cowboy in town.

It was a cold place to be.

She hadn't pushed him to let her ride the unbroken colts over the last four days. Instead, she'd come, said little and ridden the two colts he'd given her permission to ride. She'd taken to riding them out back in the round pen behind the cabin. It was far away from him and encircled by mesquite trunks to lock out distractions for the horse. In this case, it was clearly Brent who was being locked out.

When she went from barn to corral, she didn't hang around or even try to sneak a peek at what he was doing with the paint or the ornery chestnut—who'd totally and completely rebelled against everything he'd done for them so far.

He might have blamed some of his and Tacy's troubles on the fact that he hadn't gone to the churchwide Thanksgiving dinner. He hadn't been feeling particularly thankful, so he'd worked. He knew it was tomorrow that Tacy really had a problem with—the fact that he wouldn't spend Thanksgiving with his family. She would be even more furious if she knew that his mom had called again. He'd never felt so bad about saying no—because of Tacy's pushing—but he'd stuck to his guns.

Even when his mom told him that Tina had finally been given a clean bill of health by the doctors, he'd held firm…and all the while he'd had Tacy's expression of disappointment in his thoughts.

The chestnut suddenly jerked its head and swung its hips his way—as it kicked its back feet out, aiming for Brent.

Brent sidestepped and barely missed the hit as he refocused on the wild-eyed horse. Plain and simple, this horse had a streak of meanness in it. Brent had gone on autopilot while his thoughts had been on Tacy, and that was not a smart move when working with a wild card like the chestnut. Breaking this piece of rank horseflesh the gentle way might not be doable. Angry at himself and the horse, he tied the chestnut to the corral.

He needed to get his head on straight before continuing to work with this horse. If he didn't, one of them was going to get hurt.

Lugging her saddle, Tacy was leading the two colts back to the pen when she saw the chestnut try to kick Brent. Her heart stopped as only his quick sidestep saved him.

His mind wasn't on his work. *Join the crowd.*

She eyed the chestnut. He'd tied it to the fence then stalked away out the side gate and disappeared into the barn.

Tacy had done everything short of hanging a "Do Not Disturb" sign around her neck to avoid conversations with Brent. That hadn't stopped her mind from churning with thoughts and questions about him. What was she going to do about him and her feelings?

Nothing!

As always, easier said than done. That just seemed to be the theme of her life.

Feeling ornery herself, she continued to eye the chestnut as she opened the gate to the adjoining holding pen and let the black and roan loose. Brent hadn't told her to work the chestnut, said it was still too ornery.

Grabbing her saddle from where she'd dropped it on the ground as she'd let the colts go, she hiked it to her hip. Her adrenaline had begun strumming through her veins as she reached for the blanket and let herself in the gate. Quietly, she headed toward the chestnut.

Today was the day she took back her future. If Brent thought this chestnut was ornery, he hadn't seen nothin' yet.

Chapter Nineteen

❧

"Hey, girl," Tacy said gently, forcing herself to remain calm though she was feeling a rush of anticipation.

The horse's ears twitched, a sign that she wasn't sure of Tacy. She held her ground, though, and didn't move away from her. That was all the encouragement Tacy needed.

Running her hands down the soft, red coat, Tacy laid the blanket across the animal's back. Then she hiked the saddle to her hip, and with soft words, took a breath and placed the saddle over the blanket. The chestnut flinched, sidestepped, but didn't kick.

Tacy's spurs jingled with her quick steps as she moved with the fearful horse. Speaking, she reached for the cinch. She needed to hurry. Brent was in the barn, but the minute he came out and saw what she was doing, he'd blow like the punkin chunkin air cannon. Not a good thing, because with the way she was feeling she'd blow right back. It wouldn't be pretty.

With quick, expert fingers she soon had the saddle cinched and secured. Glancing around, she didn't see any sign of the cowboy and decided the smart move was to take it back out to the enclosed round pen she'd been using. With luck he wouldn't come out of the barn for a while and she'd be on its back before he heard any commotion.

Leading the way out, Tacy opened the gate and was in the middle of the open yard when she saw Brent heading her way.

One look at his face, and she knew war was about to break loose. "Tacy," he yelled. "No!"

She had a split second to make up her mind. He weighed a good seventy pounds of hard muscle more than she did, and if he wanted to tear the reins from her grasp there wasn't much she'd be able to do about it. It was time to do this.

Whether they were contained inside a

round pen or not, the time had come to take her chances on her terms.

Holding the reins tight and with one eye on Brent, Tacy reached for the saddle horn. In the same movement, her boot slid into the stirrup. Without a backward thought or glance, she lifted herself up and had just barely made it into the saddle when the chestnut kicked its hind legs and spun.

Tacy managed to secure her other boot in the stirrup and went with the spin—felt the thrill in her gut as they whirled across the yard like a rowdy twister—and then the chestnut decided to show her true colors. *The rodeo was on!*

Brent skidded to a halt. His heart was in his throat as he gauged his next move. The chestnut was as crazy as he'd thought, as unpredictable as any horse he'd ever seen—and it was bucking as hard as any world championship ride, determined to kill a cowboy's dream right there in the dust under the big lights.

But this was Tacy, here in the real world, riding like she knew what she was doing. She'd settled into the saddle and was right on point with her balance as she moved with the crazy horse.

There was no fear in her face, just exhilaration. And concentration. Clearly, she wasn't doing the ride on the cuff, hanging on for dear life—as Tina had been doing.

No, Tacy was working the ride.

And she was doing a great job!

But she was still in danger.

Brent yanked his head out of the clouds and focused on getting her off the horse in one piece—not on enjoying the show.

With a quick movement, he ducked into the horse's zone, intent on grabbing the reins. But Tacy shouted him off, yanked the reins to her far side, away from him. The movement forced the horse to turn its head away from Brent as Tacy drew its nose toward her knee. Brent dove out of the way when the horse swung its hips his way. Yanking his hat off, Brent glared at the crazy woman. She'd almost run him over. On purpose.

It hit him that she'd known what she was doing. Totally and completely. And she was still working the horse. She'd forced it to stop any forward movement because she'd pulled its head so close to her knee. Now the chestnut couldn't do anything but move in the circle as she continued to control it. As Brent watched, it gave up and came to a halt.

Not satisfied, Tacy gave over a little of her control by easing up her grip—testing the horse. The colt gave a small jump, but Tacy reined it in again, the muscles in her forearms and biceps working. He'd never noticed the strength in her pretty arms. As she pulled back and forced the animal to walk backward a few steps, he wondered what else he'd missed.

She shot Brent a look of satisfaction as the chestnut settled down. Letting the colt—and Brent—know this was no fluke, she gave the colt a gentle nudge with her spurs and walked it toward the house. Nice and easy they went. Then she turned and headed back to him.

Brent's shoulders ached with tension. Anger and pride mingled together as he watched her—but mostly anger. He held his tongue, not wanting to spook the horse again.

Tacy reined the chestnut in a step in front of him. Brent grabbed the bridle. "A word with you," he gritted through clenched teeth. Tacy swung her leg over and hopped to the ground, her eyes glinting as she handed him the reins.

"No need—they're all yours, cowboy. I'm

out of here." She tossed her hair over her shoulder and strode toward her truck.

"Not so fast," he all but yelled.

She swung around. "Hold it right there, buckaroo. You have no right to yell at me. After I get back from visiting my family, I'll be loading up and heading out. You got your wish. I'm done here—I'm gone, just as you wanted." She reached for her truck door, fumbled slightly, and seconds later drove away.

She didn't even look back at Brent in her sideview mirror.

He knew she didn't, because he was watching—too stunned by her revelation to move.

Had he gotten what he wanted?

She'd done it! And it didn't matter at all.

Gravel flying, Tacy brought her truck to a halt in the drive of Sheri's house. Men!

She was angrier than she'd ever felt and not entirely sure why. After all, she'd just experienced the most exciting ride of her life. Yet she still wanted to blow! Stalking into the house, she paused to give Birdy a gentle head rub.

"Men are impossible—and your number-one hero's the worst, Birdy. That man is as pigheaded as they come. I rode that horse like a champion. Yes, I did. You should have seen me...." Her words trailed off as she thought of what she'd just done.

As a little cowgirl growing up, she'd watched through the slats of the corral or the top rung as each of her brothers had ridden their first unruly horse. Each time her father had been standing beside her, watching his son with pride in his eyes. But that would never happen for her. Nope. She hadn't been allowed to prove that she deserved the same opportunity to win that look.

It cut deep, despite the fact that she respected that it was her father's prerogative to make that choice.

She headed to the shower, needing the hot water to ease the knots of tension from her shoulders. There wasn't water hot enough to remove the knot in her heart....

So be it. She had work at Sam's, and she needed to tell him that she was heading out. She couldn't hang around here. She would go and find a place where cowboys didn't hold against her what she was capable of. And then she'd set her dreams back on track.

Here, with Brent to distract her, she was in danger.

She might not ever see the pride in the eyes of the men she loved, but she sure wasn't sticking around to settle for less.

Nope. Cowgirls didn't cry—they didn't settle, either.

Chapter Twenty

"What do ya mean yor quitting?" Sam said, slapping his dish towel to his shoulder and giving her a scowl.

"I'm leaving. That's all. I never came here to stay. I came here to learn a trade and then go find my own place."

"But why all the sudden?" Applegate asked. He and Stanley had been on their way out of the diner. Obviously, Sam's protest had been louder than she thought.

"It's Brent, isn't it?" Stanley asked. He set the checkerboard on the bar and shook his head. "We told him he should ask you out. Not run you off."

Tacy loved these guys. "He didn't ask me

out, and he's not running me off. I'm going because it's time."

"But what about Pace comin' back and teachin' you to break them horses?"

"I've decided to head down to Salado. I had a job offer from a ranch down there and decided to come here instead. I called and they'll still hire me."

"You have a job. I hired ya," Sam said, his frown dipping even deeper. "If you need more hours, I kin give 'em to ya."

App added, "Or if ya need ranch work, then hire on around here."

"We're partial to you," Stanley said, his lips lifting briefly into a smile before deflating into a frown.

Tacy's heart tugged, looking at her buddies. "Guys, I can't stay."

"Can't or won't?" Sam asked, just as the diner's heavy door swung open and the lunch crowd started pouring in. "I have half a mind to close up shop and head out thar and give Mr. Hot Shot Cowboy a piece of my mind!"

"Let's load up," Applegate bellowed and Stanley grinned, nodding like his life depended on it.

"Fellas!" Tacy hissed, glancing at the crowd

of cowboys—Jess among them—who'd just taken their seats and tuned in to the floor show. "You will do nothing of the kind. You will behave yourselves. I'm through doing what the men in my life dictate. Including you boys, so cool your jets."

The door swung open and—as her bad timing would have it—in walked the indomitable threesome of ladies. Norma Sue led the way in front of Esther Mae and Adela. Behind them came Lacy along with several other gals who worked across the street at the candy store. Tacy was feeling some strain as everyone began greeting each other—it only took a few seconds for all the newcomers to realize that something was going on. Tacy glanced at Sam and his cohorts and just about died. They looked like they were about to go to war. She glared at them. "Stop looking like that," she whispered. Too late, Norma Sue stuffed her hands to her hips.

"What is going on? You boys ain't lookin good at all—not that you ever do."

"Tacy's leavin'," Applegate announced to the entire room. Tacy groaned and plopped a hand to the top of her head, not sure whether to pull her hair out or call a time-out!

Jess stood up, unfolded was more like it, as his eyes squinted and his face tinged purple. "Is it that bronc buster? What'd he do—break your heart?"

Tacy let her hand slide off her head and drop limply at her side. Her mouth fell open, too. "Now, Jess," she said, not exactly sure what he was thinking of doing, but it didn't look good. "You need to sit back down. If all of you must know, I'm taking a job in Salado."

"He *did* break your heart," Jess growled, threw his napkin to the table and stalked toward the door!

"Stop him!" Tacy exclaimed.

Esther Mae reacted by hopping in front of the door. She threw her arms against it, staring up at Jess. She looked like a ruffled duck in her bright yellow jogging suit. "Hold yer horses, cowboy!"

"That would probably be a good idea," Lacy said, moving to stand beside Esther Mae.

Jess glanced at Tacy. "I'll go get him and bring him to you—"

"No need," a muffled voice said as the door slowly moved forward, scooting Esther Mae gently out of the way. Brent stuck his head through the doorway. "Mind if I join the show, Esther Mae?" he asked.

"Depends on what your plans are."

Brent swept his hat off and met Tacy's gaze across the room. "That'll depend on Tacy."

"Then why are you standing out there?" Esther Mae grinned and stepped out of his way.

Tacy locked her arms across her waist and willed her clamoring heart to be still. *Not happening.*

Brent hit Jess with serious eyes that warned him to back off. Tacy held her breath as Jess shot Brent a return warning, then stepped out of the way and let him pass. Really, Jess was just full of surprises—but it looked as if maybe Brent was, too.

Hope kindled in her heart as Brent's gaze locked and held hers.

Esther Mae sighed heavily, but other than that a pin could have been heard dropping on the old wooden floors at Sam's.

"The last thing you said to me was that I got my wish." He arched a brow and cocked a half grin. "Your mind reading is off. Way off. I seem to remember when I first met you that you thought you were pretty hot stuff. Your record was one-for-one and you were too afraid of losing to chance another go at me. Now I know why. You're not nearly as smart as you think."

Tacy bit back a smile, her insides trembling. What was he doing? "How did I mess up?" she asked as he came a few more steps her way. He dropped his hat on a table.

"You didn't. You did everything right. Pushy, but right. This is one stupid meat loafer."

"Ain't that the truth," Sam ground out. Tacy shot him a glare and he grinned, raising a bushy brow above twinkling eyes that warmed her heart.

"You're not stupid," she said breathlessly.

"I'll admit I'm getting smarter every minute. You were right. I have to face my fears and you helped me. Why didn't you tell me you could do what you did on that horse?"

"You didn't ask, and—"

"What'd she do?" App demanded.

"She rode a crazy horse like a pro. That's what she did. She stuck a boot in the stirrup, settled in and took control. That's what she did. If you knew how to do that, why'd you need me? Or Pace?"

Tacy bit her lip. "I needed you to teach me the gentle way. I'm not stupid. I had a good ride today. I could've just as easily bitten the dust and you know it." Feeling more like herself, she pulled her shoulders back and strode around the counter.

He grinned. "But you didn't. You rode with no fear and with strength. But most important— you rode smart."

"So, cowboy, what exactly are you saying?" She walked to stand in front of him.

"I'm saying you got my wish wrong. I don't want you to leave. I want you to stay."

"No can do," she said, lifting her chin. "I tend to let men I love ride roughshod over me. I have to stop doing that, which means if I stick around I'd have to know you're not going to have a problem with me breaking horses."

He stepped close, his chin dipping so they were mere inches apart. "That can be arranged. You say you have this problem with the men you love?"

"That's right. If I don't love them, I can walk right over them." Chuckles rolled across the room.

"What happens if some poor cowpoke falls in love with you?"

She smiled, her toes curled with happiness. "That's one cowboy who's headed for trouble. He might want to back up and head in the other direction. When you love someone, the rules change."

Brent lifted his hands and cupped her face. Tacy shivered as her world stumbled then righted. Looking into his eyes, she felt it hold steady. "I love you, Tacy. I can't promise I won't be afraid for you, or that I won't try to keep you safe. But you have my word that I won't let my fear hold you back. You were meant to fly. I saw that today. You were beauty in motion. I liked it."

Tacy laughed as happiness bubbled up like sparkling water. "My, my, cowboy, I do believe for once you knew exactly what I wanted."

"I do love you." Brent chuckled huskily against her lips and then he kissed her. A roar went up all around them.

Tacy beamed with happiness and embarrassment as she glanced around the room. "What is wrong with you people? You act like you've never seen two people in love before."

"Oh, we've seen it plenty," Applegate said. "We jest ain't never seen two as mule-headed as the two of you."

"Boy, that's the truth," Norma Sue said.

"We thought we were going to have to hog-tie you together until y'all came to your senses."

Tacy focused on the big picture and looked up at Brent. She was so happy she didn't want to chance messing up what she'd just found—but she had a big mouth and she knew now that she had to finish what she'd started. "Speaking of coming to your senses," she said, "I'm still going home tonight so I can be home for Thanksgiving. What about you? Are you going home for Thanksgiving?"

"I am," he said. "You're right—it's time. I'm going to go home, make amends to my dad and hug my sister and my mom."

Tacy felt tears well in her eyes. "I am so happy," she said. Brent rested his forehead against hers—then she remembered there were other people in the room. But her focus was on Brent and only Brent as his arms tightened around her. This was where she'd been longing to be from almost the first moment she'd met him. "Nothing could make this day any better." She sighed. "I love you so much."

He pulled back and his lips flattened as he stared at her.

"What is it?" she asked, startled by his expression.

"I hope there is one more thing that would make you happier."

Her heart started jumping around erratically. "And what exactly would that be, cowboy?"

He grinned. "I figured after I made my peace with my family, then it'd only take two hours for me to drive down to Willow Valley to meet your family."

She feigned shock. "That brave, are you?"

Sam cleared his throat, drawing their attention. "Didn't you say yor brothers and yor daddy pert near run off anybody who came a courtin' you?"

Brent grinned. "She said that, all right. That's why I'm going—if she'll have me. I have a question I need to ask them."

"I don't know," Tacy said. "I sort of wanted to enjoy this time I have with you before the Jones brothers run you off."

Brent shook his head and tipped her chin. "Believe me, honey. I'm not going anywhere."

"Big talk," she teased. "You haven't met my brothers."

"Tacy, with you by my side I can face anything. Including the Jones brothers."

Tacy laughed. "Then come to Willow Valley. This I have to see," she said, and then she kissed him—while she could. "Poor cowboy," she whispered against his lips. "You have no idea what you're in for."

"Now there's where you're wrong, cowgirl," he said. "You and me together—we're in for the ride of our lives."

Tacy smiled against Brent's smile as her heart beat against his heart, and she knew he was absolutely, one hundred percent right!

* * * * *

Watch for Debra Clopton's next
Steeple Hill Love Inspired book,
HER FOREVER COWBOY,
coming January 2010
from Steeple Hill Books.

Dear Reader,

Hi, and welcome back to Mule Hollow! I'm so glad you decided to pick up my book and visit my sometimes crazy little town. This book came to me last summer when I was on a road trip across New Mexico heading toward Arizona. Just before the border I spotted a "Punkin Chunkin" competition going on in a pasture and instantly saw in my mind's eye Applegate and Stanley versus Norma Sue and Esther Mae in the first-ever Mule Hollow "Punkin Chunkin" competition. I really enjoyed all my research on the pumpkin tossing competitions.

I loved creating the other aspects of this story, too. Talk about two Texans almost too stubborn for their own good—Brent Stockwell and Tacy Jones weren't backing down for nothin'. Have you ever been there, done that? Boy, I have! Thankfully, God can teach us things even in our stubbornness and He can also work all things out for good—if it is His will.

I pray that you seek God's will in your life and that He rewards you for it.

I love hearing from readers and I try to respond to each one—sometimes it takes me a while because of my writing schedule and also the amount of letters and e-mails I'm receiving ☺. Thank you all so much and please know that I cherish your letters—each one boosts my spirits as I create my stories and I pray for each of you. You can reach me at Debra Clopton, P.O. Box 1125, Madisonville TX 77864 or Debraclopton.com or through Steeple Hill Books.

Until next time, live, laugh and seek God with all your heart,

Debra Clopton

P.S. I hope you'll come back to visit in January 2010 when country vet Susan Worth falls asleep at the wheel and runs straight into trouble…aka Cole Turner in *Her Forever Cowboy,* the first book in my Men of Mule Hollow miniseries.

QUESTIONS FOR DISCUSSION

1. Who was more stubborn—Tacy Jones or Brent Stockwell? Did you relate in any way to the stubbornness of the characters? Please discuss your stubborn nature.

2. Did you relate more to the older "punkin chunkin" competitors or to Brent and Tacy? Why? As humans, we do tend to dig in sometimes, don't we?

3. Have you ever had a dream you had to fight for? What was it? Have you ever had a dream you realized wasn't worth fighting for?

4. Have you ever had a dream that was worth sacrificing for something you believed was of greater value (your family's greater good, your life plan, your spouse)? Please discuss, if you feel led to.

5. At what point in the story did Tacy's heart start changing? Did she see a

greater purpose for talking Brent into teaching her to break horses?

6. In his past, Brent let his God-given talent go to his head. What had he done?

7. Drinking is such a problem and often leads to bad decisions with horrible consequences. What were the consequences of Brent's drinking?

8. Brent's dad tried to talk some sense into Brent when he was starting to let his success go to his head. How did Brent respond to that? Have you ever failed to listen to some good advice your parents tried to give you? Have you regretted being too stubborn to listen to them?

9. As a parent, have you had to watch your children making mistakes when they wouldn't listen to your advice? Have you learned something from the experience that might help someone else?

10. My verse for this book is 1 Peter 5:10: *And the God of all grace, who called you*

to His eternal glory in Christ, after you have suffered a little while, will Himself restore you and make you strong, firm and steadfast. Brent feels that he's harmed his relationship with his father beyond repair because he didn't listen to what he'd been taught and the consequences had almost cost his sister her life. God is the God of all grace and he can make us stronger after any trial we may endure. Mending earthly relationships may not be so easy, but Brent is making the right choice to go home and try. How has God made you stronger, firmer and more steadfast in your Christian walk after a trial you felt was too large to overcome?

11. Tacy realized midway through the book that she had a purpose—or responsibility as a Christian—to see if she could help Brent. It wasn't easy for her, especially since she was fighting her attraction to him, but she did it anyway. Have you ever done something you really didn't want to do even if it cost you something (time, comfort, convenience, etc.)?

12. Lacy Matlock pointed out to Tacy that sometimes a bit of stress is what is needed to make people see the light. Do you agree? Why or why not?

13. Tacy's father didn't want to teach her to break horses, and yet he did not keep her from going to learn from someone else. Does this make sense to you? Why or why not?

14. Patience is a virtue that most of us could use more of. I know I need more of it, just as Brent and Tacy both needed it. Can you pass along any helpful tips on patience to the group? What has God taught you through the development of patience?

*Here's a sneak peek at
"Merry Mayhem" by Margaret Daley,
one of the two riveting suspense
stories in the new collection
CHRISTMAS PERIL,
available in December 2009
from Love Inspired Suspense.*

"Run. Disappear… Don't trust anyone, especially the police."

Annie Coleman almost dropped the phone at her ex-boyfriend's words, but she couldn't. She had to keep it together for her daughter. Jayden played nearby, oblivious to the sheer terror Annie was feeling at hearing Bryan's gasped warning.

"Thought you could get away," a gruff voice she didn't recognize said between punches. "You haven't finished telling me what I need to know."

Annie panicked. What was going on? What was happening to Bryan on the other end? Confusion gripped her in a choke hold, her chest tightening with each inhalation.

"I don't want—" Bryan's rattling gasp punctuated the brief silence "—any money. Just let me go. I'll forget everything."

"I'm not worried about you telling a soul." The menace in the assailant's tone underscored his deadly intent. "All I need to know is exactly where you hid it. If you tell me now, it will be a lot less painful."

"I can't—" Agony laced each word.

"What's that? A phone?" the man screamed.

The sounds of a struggle then a gunshot blasted her eardrum. Curses roared through the connection.

Fear paralyzed Annie in the middle of her kitchen. Was Bryan shot? Dead?

The voice on the phone returned. "Who's this? Who are you?"

The assailant's voice so clear on the phone panicked her. She slammed it down onto its cradle as though that action could sever the memories from her mind. But nothing would. Had she heard her daughter's father being killed? What information did Bryan have? Did that man know her name? Question after question bombarded her from all sides, but inertia held her still.

The ringing of the phone jarred her out of her trance. Her gaze zoomed in on the lighted panel on the receiver and saw the call was from Bryan's cell. The assailant had her home telephone number. He could discover where she lived. He knew what she'd heard.

"Mommy, what's wrong?"

Looking up at Jayden, Annie schooled her features into what she hoped was a calm expression while her stomach reeled. "You know, I've been thinking, honey, we need to take a vacation. It's time for us to have an adventure. Let's see how fast you can pack." Although she tried to make it sound like a game, her voice quavered, and Annie curled her trembling hands until her fingernails dug into her palms.

At the door, her daughter paused, cocking her head. "When will we be coming back?"

The question hung in the air, and Annie wondered if they'd ever be able to come back at all.

* * * * *

*Follow Annie and Jayden as they flee to
Christmas, Oklahoma, and hide from
a killer—with a little help from
a small-town police officer.*

*Look for CHRISTMAS PERIL by
Margaret Daley and Debby Giusti,
available December 2009
from Love Inspired Suspense.*

Love Inspired®
SUSPENSE
RIVETING INSPIRATIONAL ROMANCE

These contemporary tales
of intrigue and romance
feature Christian characters
facing challenges to their faith...
and their lives!

**Four new Love Inspired Suspense titles are
available every month wherever books are
sold, including most bookstores, supermarkets,
drug stores and discount stores.**

Steeple
Hill®

Visit:
www.steeplehillbooks.com

Love Inspired.
HISTORICAL
INSPIRATIONAL HISTORICAL ROMANCE

Engaging stories of romance,
adventure and faith,
these novels are set in
various historical periods
from biblical times
to World War II.

NOW AVAILABLE!

Steeple Hill®